Enriching Your Competence in English

Prescribed for TYBA Compulsory English
University of Pune

Ashok Thorat

Balchandra Valke

Shridhar Gokhale

Orient Longman

Acknowledgements

For permission to use copyright material, the editors and publishers wish to thank Ward Lock Ltd. London, for 'Leg Break' from *How to Play Cricket* by Ian Morrison; Pocket Books, New York, for a pasage from *Roget's Pocket Thesaurus*; Wren and Martin for imprint page from *High School Grammar and Composition*; OUP, Oxford, for the table of contents from *A Theory of Linguistic Sign* by Keller Rudy. and an extract from *Pride and Prejudice* by Jane Austen ed. by James Kingsley; OUP, New Delhi, for graphs from *Public Report on Basic Education in India;* OUP, Mumbai, for a passage from 'All About a Dog' by A.G Gardiner from *Poetry and Minor Forms of English Literature* edited by Ashok Thorat and others; Orient Paperbacks, Delhi, for the foreword from *Kanthapura* by Raja Rao; B.I. Publications, Chennai, for the back page from *Wole Soyinka: A Quest for Renewal* by David M.T; B P B Publication, New Delhi, for a paragraph from *Mastering the Internet* by Glee Harrah Cady and Pat Mc Gregor; Sterling Publishers for a Chart on 'Distribution of World Population' from *Fundamentals of Population Geography* by B N Ghosh; the NCERT for graphs from *General Geography of India*; World Book Inc. Chicago, for 'How a Digital Computer Works' and 'How flour is Milled' from *The World Book Encyclopedia*; Concept Publishing Company, New Delhi, for a piechart from *The Textbook of Practical Geography* by Md. Zulfequar Ahmed Khan; the University of Pune for graphs from the 47th Annual Report and a passage from University News; the Reserve Bank of India for a chart on 'Industrywise Profit Margin'; Heinemann Educational Books Ltd. London, for a passage from *The Commonsense of Science* by J. Brownowski; the Publications Division, Government of India, New Delhi, for a passage on 'Education' by S. Radhakrishnan; Macmillan for a passage from 'Dangers of Drug Addicts' by Hardin B Jones from *Prose for the Young Reader* ed by D K. Sebastian; the Centre for the Study of Democratic Institutions Intergroup Incorporated, New York, for passages from 'An Inventory of Disaster' by Paul R Ehrlich and John P Holdren from *Ecocide and Thoughts Toward Survival* by Clifton Fadiman and Jean White; *The Times of India* for 'Tendulkar's 25 centuries', 'Better Information, Better Health' and an 'Interview with V S Naipaul'.

ORIENT LONGMAN PRIVATE LIMITED

Registered Office
3-6-752 Himayatnagar, Hyderabad 500 029 (A. P.), INDIA
e-mail : cogeneral@orientlongman.com

Other Offices
Bangalore, Bhopal, Bhubaneshwar, Chandigarh,
Chennai, Ernakulam, Guwahati, Hyderabad, Jaipur,
Kolkata, Lucknow, Mumbai, New Delhi, Patna

First Printed 2000
Reprinted 2001, 2002 (twice), 2003, 2004, 2005, 2006, 200[illegible]
ISBN 81 250 1900 6

Typeset at
Devi Information Systems
Chennai 600 029.

Printed in India at
Sujata Printers
Mumbai 400 013.

Published by
Orient Longman Private Limited
R. Kamani Marg, Mumbai 400 001.

e-mail : mumgeneral@orientlongman.com

INTRODUCTION

The aim of this coursebook is to enrich students' competence in English by enabling them to perform various tasks using English more efficiently and confidently. The book has a practical orientation and is expected to have an immediate application in the students' lives. This functional aspect is reflected in the large number of exercises included here. It needs to be mentioned that answers to these exercises can be refined and students need to develop the skill of reading their own answers critically and improving them in a continuous process throughout the academic year. The exercises should be seen as samples, and teachers and students are welcome to devise more exercises on similar lines. This book is designed to interest students with various degrees of competence in English. If they carry out various tasks specified, they will be able to enhance both their own linguistic skills of listening, speaking, reading and writing and also their reference skills.

The different units should not be merely looked upon as 'lessons' that have to be 'finished'. They should be seen as 'springboards' for successful communication.

Finally, it needs to be mentioned that even if this coursebook is divided into units, language learning and teaching should be seen as integrated activities involving amalgamation of various skills and sub-skills.

ASHOK THORAT
BALCHANDRA VALKE
SHRIDHAR GOKHALE

CONTENTS

VOCABULARY

Introduction

Words are the building blocks of language, whereas grammar functions as the cement that holds the blocks together. Mastery over a language is possible only if we have satisfactory command over both vocabulary and grammar. The aim of this unit is to enable you to improve your word power.

a. How many words do we know?

In general, it is true to say that the more words we know, the more efficient we are in the use of a language. If we know very few words in a language, we are likely to manage with the words we know and that necessarily means using inappropriate words or using more words to convey the same meaning.

b. How many meanings does a word have?

Most words in a dictionary have two or more meanings. When we think that we know a word, we may in fact know only a few of the possible meanings. All of you know the word 'cool'. How many distinct meanings of this word do you know?

Exercise A

The following are some sentences in which the word 'cool' has occurred. Think about the meaning of the word in each context.

1. Everyone likes to enjoy a cool breeze in the evening.
2. My boss didn't help me. In fact, he was very cool towards me.
3. He was not disturbed when he received the sad news. On the contrary, he was calm and cool.
4. She looks very cool in her new dress.
5. The room was painted in a cool colour.

Even if you have been able to guess the possible meanings in the contexts given, that is perfectly all right. Check the meanings you have guessed by referring to a good dictionary, particularly a dictionary that gives you usage. (Such a dictionary gives you at least a few sentences illustrating how words are actually used in different contexts.) Remember that the ability to guess meanings is as important as your knowledge of words.

c. How can we improve our vocabulary?

Like other aspects of language, vocabulary can be improved by consistent hard work. You need not check every unfamiliar word in a dictionary but when you feel that some of the unfamiliar words are very important in the context in which they have occurred, it is necessary to refer to a good dictionary and find out the relevant meaning. If an unfamiliar word is repeated frequently in a piece of writing or if it occurs in the title of a chapter or section, it obviously suggests that understanding that unknown word is very important.

We must form the habit of making good use of the dictionary. A dictionary generally gives us the following types of information about words—pronunciation, spelling, part of speech (grammatical category), meaning, usage (sentences illustrating the uses of the word), related words, phrases and idioms, use in specific contexts (labels like formal, colloquial, American English, archaic, rare and technical). The system used by each dictionary for indicating these different types of information is explained at the beginning of the dictionary. We should read those pages if we wish to make maximum use of the dictionary.

Exercise B

Refer to the following words in a good dictionary. Read and try to understand all the information given in it about each word.

density	elucidate	fruition	hegemony	
inherent	mealy-mouthed	mission	outlook	sectarian

Instead of studying a word in isolation, it is desirable to study different forms of the words together. By adding different suffixes to a word, we are able to convert it into a noun, verb, adjective or adverb. By adding different prefixes, we can modify the meaning of a word. For example, when you study the word 'prohibit', it is useful to pay attention to its derived forms like prohibition (n), prohibitive (adj) and prohibitory (adj). This eventually saves our time and makes us more efficient users of the language.

Exercise C

Complete the following table. In some cases, a particular form of a word may not be available. Refer to a dictionary and check your answers.

Noun	Verb	Adjective	Adverb
		prescriptive	
	explain		
respect			
			reliably
	construct		
contradiction			
	reduce		
			actively
		peaceful	
		clear	
courage			

Like human beings, words also prefer a particular company. That is, a particular word tends to occur in the company of certain other words and not just any word. For example, the word, 'duty' is preceded by the verb 'do' or 'perform' and not 'make'. We can say 'do one's duty' or 'perform one's duty' but not 'make one's duty'. This is referred to as collocation. There is no logical reason why we cannot use the expression 'make one's duty'. Collocations are purely conventional. In order to improve our vocabulary, we must know the collocations of words. If we try to literally translate from our first language into English, we are likely to make errors of collocations.

Consider the following examples.

'commit a crime' and not 'do a crime'
'a big mistake' and not a 'a large mistake'
'a golden opportunity' and not 'a silver opportunity'
'make amends' and not 'do amends'
'a high standard' and not 'a great standard'
'a good intention' and not 'a nice intention'
'a hot favourite ' and not 'a warm favourite' or ' a cold favourite'
'innermost feelings' and not 'innermost expectations'
'cheap popularity' and not 'inexpensive popularity'

The difference between a competent user of a language and an incompetent user lies in the ability to understand the right collocations of a word. We need to be very careful about collocations and we should refer to a dictionary even if we have the slightest doubt.

Exercise D

1. *Make phrases using an adjective before the nouns given below. Refer to a dictionary and check your answers.*

idea	expectations	problem	shortage	opposition
delay	advice	wages	poem	mountain

2. *Make phrases using appropriate verbs before the nouns given below. Refer to a dictionary and check your answers.*

support	results	operation	money	fame
service	correction	calculation	clarification	solution

In order to improve our vocabulary it is necessary to know synonyms and antonyms. Synonyms are words with similar meanings and antonyms are words with opposite meanings. For example, 'exact' 'precise' and 'accurate' are synonyms, whereas 'precise' and 'imprecise' or 'vague' are antonyms. Of course, we must remember that even if synonyms have largely similar meanings they are not totally interchangeable. That is, they cannot always be used in identical contexts due to collocational restrictions. For example, we can say 'a beautiful girl' or 'a pretty girl'. We can say ' a beautiful picture', but we can never say ' a pretty picture'.

Lexical Sets

If we take a particular subject matter or area of knowledge, we find that a large number of words are interrelated. One way of improving vocabulary is to group words together according to topics and learn them. Such groups of words are called lexical sets.

The following words and phrases are some of the members of the lexical set 'traffic'.

heavy traffic, traffic jam, crowd, vehicle, road, corner, turn, traffic lights, policeman, licence, traffic sense, transport, peak hour, rules and regulations, travel, journey, highway, lanes, by-lanes

The following are some words and phrases which are members of the lexical set 'cricket'.

pitch, umpire, team, player, batsman, bowler, wicket-keeper, score-board, mid-on, boundary line, sixer, run-out, record, commentator,one-dayer, test match, highlights, presentations

The following are some words and phrases which are members of the lexical set 'cooking'.

kitchen, utensil, pressure cooker, mixer, refrigerator, spice, vegetable, fruit, chopper-board, slice, knife, spoon, sift, mix, peel, roll out, crush, mash, squeeze, sprinkle, tasty, delicious, hot, serve, lunch, dinner, breakfast, dining-table.

Exercise E

Add as many words as you can to the three lexical sets given above. Write as many words and phrases belonging to the following lexical sets as possible.

nature	education	career	home	holiday
clothes	computer	happiness	sorrow	leisure

Compare your list with your friends' lists and add as many words and phrases as possible to your own list. You will notice that sometimes there is an overlap among lexical sets. That is, a particular word may belong to two or more lexical sets. Very often, lexical sets give unity to a paragraph or a piece of writing.

Exercise F

Read the following extract from a short story by K A Abbas. Identify from the passage words and phrases related to 'rain'. The story is entitled 'The Sparrows.' Find out as many words and phrases related to sparrows as possible.

One monsoon evening, when the sky was overcast with threatening clouds, Rahim Khan returned from the fields a little earlier than usual. He found a group of children playing on the road. They ran away as they saw him, and even left their shoes behind in their haste. In vain did Rahim Khan shout, 'Why are you running away? I am not going to beat you'. Meanwhile, it had started drizzling and he hurried homewards to tie up the bullocks before the big downpour came.

Entering his hut, Rahim Khan lighted the earthenware oil lamp and placed some crumbs of bread for the sparrows before he prepared his own dinner. 'O Nuru! O Bundu!' he shouted, but the sparrows did not come out. Anxious to find out what had happened to his friends, he peered into the nest and found the quartet scared and sitting huddled up within their feathers. At the very spot where the nest lay, the roof was leaking. Rahim Khan took a ladder and went in the pouring rain to repair the damage. By the time the job was satisfactorily done he was thoroughly drenched. As he sat on the cot, Rahim Khan sneezed, but he did not heed the warning and went to sleep. Next morning he awoke with a high fever.

Processes of Word Formation

In order to improve our mastery of vocabulary, it is necessary to understand how longer words are formed from shorter words by adding certain elements and also how sometimes words are made by combining two independent words or by shortening a longer word.

The most common method of forming words in English is to add some elements before or after the base word. The word which is the smallest unit of meaning is called the base. For example, the word 'room' is a base because it cannot be divided any further into meaningful units, but the word 'friendly' is not the base because it can be divided into two meaningful units—'friend' and-'ly'. We can not say that 'friend' is the base and the element '-ly' has been added to it. Similarly, the word 'preview' is not a base because it can be divided into two meaningful units—'pre' and 'view'. The word 'view' is the base and the element 'pre-' has been added before it. Elements like 'pre-' which are added before the base are called prefixes and the elements like '-ly' which are added after the base are called suffixes. Each prefix and suffix has its own meaning and if we know these meanings, we can easily guess the meanings of even unknown words.

The following are some important prefixes and suffixes in English. Their approximate meanings are given below along with a few words illustrating them.

Some Important Prefixes

1. ambi – two, both, double	ambivalent, ambiguous
2. anti – opposite, against	anti-war, anti-rust
3. auto – self	autopump, autobiography
4. bi – two, double	bi-weekly, bisect
5. bio – concerning life	biology, biography
6. chron – concerning time	chronology, chronic
7. co – with, together	co-worker, co-operate, co-pilot
8. con – together	contact, conference
9. counter – against, opposite	counter-attack, counterfoil
10. de – remove, reduce	decentralise, devaluation

11. dis – showing negative or opposite	discontinue, dishonest, disrespect
12. extra – beyond	extra-constitutional, extra-marital
13. hyper – more than usual	hypertension, hypersensitive
14. inter – between	international, inter-departmental
15. micro – small	microscope, microprocessor
16. mini – small	mini-skirt, minimise, mini-lunch
17. mis – badly or wrongly	misrepresent, misinformation
18. mono – one, single	monotonous, monologue
19. non – showing negative	non-co-operation, non-smoker
20. out – beyond, further	outstanding, outshine, outgrow
21. over – too much, above, additional	overpopulation, overtime, overcoat
22. post – after	post-war, post-mortem, postpone
23. pre – before	pre-marital, preview, prepare
24. pro – for, in favour of	pro-American, Pro-Vice-Chancellor
25. re – again	rewrite, repeat, review, restatement
26. semi – half, partial	semi-circle, semi-darkness
27. sub – below, under, less important	sub-zero, sub-inspector, subordinate
28. super – above, more	superfast, superordinate
29 tele – distant	television, teleprinter
30. un – showing negative or opposite	unnoticed, unlucky, unwanted
31. under – very little	underdeveloped, underestimate
32. vice – person next in rank	vice-captain, Vice-Chancellor

Some Important Suffixes

1. -able/ -ible – having the quality of something that can be (-ed)	readable, comfortable, permissible
2. -al – concerning something	historical, political
3. -an/-ian – person connected with something	Indian, electrician, musician, historian
4. -ance/ -ence – action, quality or condition of something	tolerance, transference, resistance, patience
5. -ancy/ -ency–quality or condition of something	transparency, expectancy urgency
6. -ant/ -ent – something or someone that—	resistant, recipient, claimant
7. -ar – concerning something	muscular, circular, molecular
8. -cide – killing someone/ something	insecticide, suicide, pesticide
9. -cy – the quality of being—	privacy, accuracy
10. -ee – someone who is (-ed)	payee, employee, examinee
11. -en – (adjective) made of, (verb) to make	golden, silken, lighten, darken
12. -er/ -or – someone who does something	teacher, player, governor, director, manager
13. -ess – the female of—	lioness, actress
14. -free – without—	sugarfree, tax-free, rent-free
15. -ful – having the quality of—	beautiful, faithful, wonderful
16. -gamy – marriage to the number or kind of people stated	polygamy, monogamy
17. -hood – the condition or time of being a—	childhood, adulthood, likelihood

18. -ic – connected with	psychic, photographic
19. -ify – make or become—	solidify, magnify, specify
20. -ion – the condition of being—	satisfaction, stratification, junction
21. -ise/ize/ – make	idolise, regularise, crystallise
22. -ish – belonging to a nation or having the quality of (used pejoratively)	Irish, slavish, childish
23. -ism – belief in the principle/ philosophy of; having the quality of	communism, monism, mammonism heroism
24. -ist – person believing in the principle/ philosophy of; studying the specified subject	communist, fadist linguist, physicist, chemist
25. -ity – having the quality of	regularity, profundity, specificity
26. -less – without-–	careless, speechless, childless
27. -let – small size of—	booklet, pamphlet
28. -logy – scientific study of—	geology, phonology
29. -ment – act or result of—	acknowledgment, management, government
30. -ness – condition of being—	goodness, carefulness, kindness
31. -ocracy – government of—	democracy, bureaucracy
32. -ous – having the quality of—	porous, mischievous, dangerous
33. -proof – not having the effect of—	rust-proof, sound-proof, leak-proof
34. -ship – having the position or skill of	lecturership, kingship, penmanship
35. -y – full of or typical of—	windy, cloudy, starry, rainy

In some cases, the prefix or suffix can be easily separated from the base. For example, in the word 'rewrite', the prefix 're' can be separated from the base 'write', but in a word like 'prepare', the prefix 'pre' cannot be separated from 'pare', because pare is not an independent base in English. However, it is still useful to know that the prefix 'pre' has the meaning of 'before' even in the word 'prepare'. A good way of improving your vocabulary is to try to identify prefixes and suffixes and relate them to their meanings.

Exercise G

Identify the prefixes and suffixes used in the following words and try to understand the meanings of the words.

prefabricated	restatement	misunderstanding	disallowed
specificity	dishonesty	disinterestedness	anti-war
infrequently	inaccessible	impossibility	unnoticed
non-commercial	computerised	tabular	unidentified
carelessness	descriptively	mismanagement	formulations
economist	sociological	vice-captain	apolitical
privatisation	clarifications	independence	booklet
modernity	anti-American	interdepartmental	daily
unparliamentary	internationalisation		

Another common method of forming words in English is to combine two or more bases. For example, in the word 'classroom' we have two bases— class and room. Each of them can be used independently as a word. Such words are called compound words.

Examples of compound nouns:
class teacher, art gallery, postcard, night lamp, poet-critic, mother-in-law, airbus

Examples of compound adjectives:
sky blue, bullet-proof, hand-washed, long-awaited

Examples of compound verbs:
whitewash, spring clean

Sometimes a word belonging to a particular part of speech is used as another part of speech and it gets established in the language. For example, the word 'bottle' was originally a noun in English, but later it came to be used as a verb. The same happened to the words 'motor' and 'cash' as exemplified by the following sentences.

Cold drinks are *bottled* in this factory.

They *motored* the distance in about five hours.

I have not *cashed* the cheque yet.

Similarly, the auxiliary verb 'must' is often used as a noun in modern English. For example,

Hard work is a *must* for success.

Sometimes two bases are combined in a word as in compounding, but the word retains only a part of one or both the words. Such words are called 'blends'. For example, the word 'medicare' is a combination of 'medical' and 'care', but only a part of the word medical is retained in the blend. The word 'brunch' is a combination of the words 'breakfast' and 'lunch' and only some part of each of the two words is retained.

Exercise H

Identify the two words which are blended in the following examples.

smog	appetingling	edutainment	smoodles

Words Often Confused

The right choice of words contributes significantly to an effective use of vocabulary. Therefore, we should be particularly careful in the use of the words which are often confused.

Words may be confused due to the similarity of spelling or pronunciation. The following are some of the words confused in this manner. Their meanings are given and they are used in sentences so as to bring out the difference between them.

1. **accept** and **except**

'Accept' is a verb, whereas 'except' is a preposition. 'Accept' means 'take', but 'except' means 'not including'.

The manager refused to *accept* the agency's offer, because he thought that it was not in the best interests of his company.

Everyone *except* the manager attended the function.

2. **affect** and **effect**

Both are verbs. 'Affect' means 'influence in an undesirable manner' and 'effect' means 'implement or put into practice'

Heavy smoking has *affected* his lungs.

The government has not yet *effected* the new policy that it announced last week.

3. **illusion** and **allusion**

Both the words are used as nouns. 'Illusion', means 'a false idea or impression', whereas 'allusion' means 'reference'.

I have no *illusions* about myself. I know my limitations well.

He made an *allusion* to some events from the Mahabharata.

4. **award** and **reward**

Both the words are used as nouns and verbs. An 'award' is a prize or money given as a result of an official decision, whereas 'reward' is a kind of return for something noble or good done by a person.

My friend has won many *awards* in quiz-competitions.

As a *reward* for her sincerity and honesty, the maid was presented with a sari.

5. **ceremonial** and **ceremonious**

Both the words are adjectives. 'Ceremonial' means 'as a part of a ceremony', whereas 'ceremonious' means 'very formal or polite'.

The bride looked very beautiful in her *ceremonial* dress.

The organiser was too *ceremonious* in proposing a vote of thanks.

6. **compliment** and **complement**

Both the words are nouns. The word 'compliment' means 'greeting', whereas the word 'complement' refers to 'something which completes something else'.

My friend received many *compliments* on his grand success.
Fruits are a good *complement* to leafy vegetables.

7. **imaginary** and **imaginative**

Both the words are adjectives. 'Imaginary' means 'unreal'. It describes something which is a product of imagination. 'Imaginative' means 'full of imagination' and it is generally used to describe a person.

The story is set in an *imaginary* land.
Scientists and artists are highly *imaginative* people.

8. **judicial** and **judicious**

Both the words are adjectives. 'Judicial' means 'concerned with law', whereas 'judicious' means 'thoughtful' or 'prudent'.

Judicial procedures often involve delays.
My friend was very *judicious* in choosing his career.

9. **principal** and **principle**

Both the words are nouns. 'Principal' means 'the head of the organisation or institution'. As an adjective the word also means 'main' or 'important'. A 'principle' is a moral, a rule or set of ideas, which controls behaviour.

My friend was recently appointed *Principal* of a college.
We must all follow the *principle* of religious tolerance.

10. **superficial** and **superfluous**

Both the words are adjectives. 'Superficial' means 'related to the surface' but 'superfluous' means 'unnecessary'.

Many students have only a *superficial* knowledge of the subject that they study.
Since the train is never full, the reservations are *superfluous*.

11. **childish** and **childlike**

Both the words are adjectives. The word 'childish' is used in a pejorative or critical sense, whereas the word 'childlike' is used appreciatively.

Everyone laughed at his *childish* questions.

Many authors have written about the *childlike* simplicity of villagers.

12. **historic** and **historical**

Both are adjectives. The world 'historic' refers to something which is memorable in history, whereas 'historical' is something related to history.

The minister's visit to Japan was a *historic* one.

The historian is interested in offering *historical* evidence for his claims.

13. **advice** and **advise**

The former of these words is a noun and the latter a verb.

Whenever I need some *advice*, I consult my grandfather.

The teacher has *advised* me to study poetry before attempting to be a poet.

Another similar pair of words is 'practice' and 'practise'

Exercise I

The following are some more pairs of words often confused. Use a good dictionary for reference and distinguish between them.

legible and eligible	eminent and imminent
industrial and industrious	ingenious and ingenuous
sensible and sensitive	practical and practicable
official and officious	momentary and momentous
later and latter	graceful and gracious
envy and jealousy	discover and invent
discrete and discreet	

GRAMMAR

Introduction

We must not study grammar in isolation. It must be related to different tasks that we need to perform in day-to-day life. The topics of grammar included in this unit are advanced topics and mastery in these areas would indicate a high level of competence in the use of English. In the topic 'revision', an attempt has been made to give students more practice in some of the most problematic areas of grammar. There are exercises in the form of isolated sentences, but wherever possible, they are also in the form of short texts. The aim of the latter is to bring grammar closer to life. The exercises given here are sample exercises. Students and teachers should attempt more exercises from other grammar books for additional practice in problematic areas.

Phrasal Verbs

One way of improving our vocabulary is to try to have mastery over what are called phrasal verbs. A phrasal verb is a group of words consisting of a verb along with an adverb or a preposition and its meaning cannot often be understood by understanding the meaning of the verb and the adverb or preposition separately. For example, 'look after', 'look for', 'look into' and 'look forward to' are four different phrasal verbs. Consider the following sentences.

It is the duty of the society to *look after* old people.

She was *looking for* her lost pen.

The Principal has promised to *look into* the complaint .

I *look forward* to visiting Japan next year.

From these sentences you can easily guess the meaning of the four phrasal verbs. 'Look after' means 'take care of', 'look for' means 'try to find out' 'look into' means 'attend to' and 'look forward to' means 'to be excited about some future action'.

Many common verbs like 'do', 'make', 'give', 'take', 'put', 'run' and 'come' are combined with adverbs or prepositions to form phrasal verbs. It is useful to look up all the phrasal verbs listed under such verbs in a good dictionary and pay attention to their meanings and usage.

The following are different phrasal verbs involving the verb 'give'.

give back – return something to a person

give in – accept one's defeat

give off – produce a smell, light, sound etc

give out – distribute, announce

give up – stop doing something

give up on – stop hoping that someone will do something

give up to – allow oneself to be carried away by some emotion

Exercise A

Use the phrases given above in the following sentences to fill in the blanks.

1. You shouldn't have________ my address to everyone.
2. She has failed three times in the examination and her parents ________ her now.
3. Difficulties test your resourcefulness and you should not ________so easily.
4. The surgery ________ his power of speech.
5. The candle ________cool and pleasant light.
6. The doctors have finally persuaded him to ________ smoking.
7. Since he lost his parents, he __________himself _________ frustration.

The following are some more phrasal verbs, with their meanings and they are also used in sentences.

account for – explain something satisfactorily

Your letter does not *account for* your delay in despatching the goods.

bear out – confirm/support something

The experiment *bears out* my hypothesis that the two chemicals have contrary effects.

call for – require, demand

The situation *calls for* immediate corrective action on the part of the management.

catch up with – to improve/work hard so that you reach the same standard as others

She has missed the first three months of the term. She must work harder to *catch up* with the rest of the class.

Exercise B

Find out the meanings of the following phrasal verbs and use them in sentences so as to bring out their meaning. Refer to a good dictionary for both meanings and usage.

back someone up	break down	fall back on
call on	get over	go back on
go through	hang on to	hold on
keep up	lead up to	let down
live up to	look up to	put off
make up one's mind	put up with	run into
see through	set in	stand for
be taken aback	turn down	

Prepositions

This is often regarded as the most complicated topic in grammar. The reason is that the choice of a preposition in a particular context is often governed by convention and cannot be explained by any logical rule.

Consider the following examples.

Yesterday we discussed the students' problems.

Yesterday we had a discussion on the students' problems.

You may have noticed that no preposition is used after the verb 'discuss' in the first sentence, but the preposition 'on' is used after the noun 'discussion' in the second sentence. We cannot rewrite the first sentence, using the preposition 'on'.

Yesterday we discussed on the students' problems. (✗)

There is no logical explanation for the use or non-use of prepositions in the sentences given above. It entirely depends on the practice prevalent among the native users of English. The best way of improving our competence in the use of prepositions is to check the usage given in any good dictionary. If you check the usage of 'discuss' and 'discussion' in a dictionary, it would clearly guide you in the use of prepositions.

Another reason for the difficulty in using prepositions is the fact that in some contexts two or more prepositions are equally correct and there is no difference of meaning. For example,

My approach is different *from* yours.

My approach is different *to* yours.

I have already spoken *to* the director.

I have already spoken *with* the director.

Though both 'speak to' and 'speak with' are equally acceptable in British English, 'speak to' is used more frequently than 'speak with' in British English. However, 'speak with' is used more frequently than 'speak to' in General American English.

Sometimes the usage of prepositions undergoes a slight change. For example, consider the difference between *between* and *among*. Conventionally *between* is used to refer to two objects or persons and *among* for three or more objects or persons. For example,

Mother divided the cake *between* the two children.

Mother divided the cake *among* the four children.

However, the usage has been gradually changing. In modern British English, it is possible to say

Mother divided the cake *between* the four children.

In modern British English, *between* is used to refer to two or more objects or persons. But interestingly, the usage of *among* has not changed. It still refers to three or more objects or persons.

As we have seen earlier, prepositions play a major role in phrasal verbs. A phrasal verb sometimes consists of a verb and a preposition and the meaning of the phrasal verb is not the collective meaning of the verb and that of the preposition. Sometimes a change of preposition brings about a change in the meaning of a sentence.

In some cases, the use of a preposition is tied up with the use of an article. For example,

We went to Mumbai *by* car.

We went to Mumbai *in* a car.

We have to use the expressions 'by car' and 'in a car'.We cannot use the expressions 'by a car' or 'in car'. The same applies to expressions like 'by train' and 'in a train' and 'by plane' and 'in a plane'.

Exercise C

1. Explain the difference in meaning between the following pairs of sentences. If you have any doubts, refer to a good dictionary or consult your teacher.

1. The boy jumped on the fence.
   The boy jumped over the fence.

2. There is a calendar over the fire-place.
   There is a calendar above the fire-place.

3. The Principal looked at the complaint.
   The Principal looked into the complaint.
   The Principal looked for the complaint.

4. I shall meet you at Satara.
   I shall meet you in Satara.

5. He got into the bus at the first bus-stop.
   He got off the bus at the first bus-stop.

6. I visited the hospital with my mother.
   I visited the hospital for my mother.

7. When I looked through the window of the aeroplane, I saw clouds under us.
   When I looked through the window of the aeroplane, I saw clouds below us.

8. The man in the blue shirt is my friend.
   The man with the blue shirt is my friend.

9. They reached the railway station in time.
   They reached the railway station on time.

10. Students need to submit the assignment on Monday.
    Students need to submit the assignment by Monday.

2. *Fill in the blanks in the following sentences using appropriate prepositions. Refer to a dictionary or consult your teacher for the correct answers.*

1. The cloth available in this market is superior ________ what is available elsewhere.
2. I waited ______ the guests ________ the entrance________the railway station.
3. I have been studying English ________1995.
4. We have been playing cricket ________the last ten years.
5. I met him ________ the first time ________ board the ship.
6. Students are certainly capable ________ independent work.
7. I am not aware ________ any such complaints made ________ the past.
8. I was greatly pleased ________ myself when I read the poem again.
9. We must be proud ________ the glorious past ________ our country..
10. My sister is fond _________ watching the changing shapes ________ the clouds.
11. I must apologise _________ you ________ the inordinate delay ________ starting the construction.
12. Beware ________ the dog!
13. The product you have sent us does not conform ________ the specifications ________ our order.
14. When we go abroad, we must behave ________ conformity ________ the laws ________ that country.
15. The post office is just ________ the school.
16. If you persist ________ finding fault with others, you will make yourself very unpopular.
17. Please refer ________ the latest circular _______ an update ________ this topic.

18. We must never resort ________ unfair means to achieve our objectives.

19. It never occurred ________ him to lodge a complaint.

20. There is no probability ________ him changing his decision.

21. This property belongs ________ my closest friend.

22. The manager prevented him ________ applying ________ the new job.

23. This was never expected ________ my best friends.

24. He left the hall all ________ once ________ talking ________ anyone.

25. We are submitting the report ________ accordance ________ the legal requirements.

26. The celebrity was conspicuous _____ the function ______ his absence.

27. When the drum was heated, it suddenly burst ________ flames.

28. Some people always fret ________ something or the other.

29. The film pays homage ________ Satyajit Ray.

30. We first took the lift up ________ third floor.

31. Please submit an outline ________ your main argument.

32. We have decided to keep ________ the plan and complete all the work ________ record-time.

33. The discussion has raised hopes ___________ an early settlement ________ the issue.

34. ________ reference ________ your recent advertisement, I would like to apply ________ the post ________ an accounts clerk.

35. I was _________ the edge ________ my seat when the two actors started arguing.

36. The unknown gunman sprayed the crowd ________ bullets.

37. His mood often swung ________ deep despair ________ great joy.

38. The workers think very highly ________ the boss.

39. The injured man tossed _______ pain ________ side ________ side.

40. The actor is uniquely suited ________ the role that he is playing.

41. When I heard the news, I felt ________ top ________ the world.

42. The volunteers looked _______ the wreckage ________ any survivors.

43. She was wearing the same colour ________ me.

44. Please switch ____________ if you don't like this television programme .

45. You must not lose your sleep ________ this problem.

46. The government wants to introduce restraints ________ spending money ________ marriages.

47. Tears oozed out ________his eyelids.

48. We were greatly impressed ________ her oratory.

49. I am guilty ________ forgetting your birthday again.

50. It is customary _________ the chairperson to sit _____ the head_______ the table.

3. *Fill in the blanks in the following passages, using appropriate prepositions.*

1. Whenever I have a doubt __________ the meaning or usage ________ a word, I shall make it a point to refer ________ the dictionary. ________ the dictionary there is also a brief section ________ word-building.

2. The governments ________ many countries have been spending a lot ________ the propagation ________ the concept ________ family planning. Attempts are being made ________ a massive scale to convince people that it is much better to have only one or two children and to be able to provide them ________ the best ________ things ________ life. The government ________ India offers attractive incentives ________ those undergoing family planning operations. Various family planning devices are now available ________ highly subsidised prices. The government may even think ________ punitive action ________ those who have more ________ two children. China insists ________ couples having only one child.

3. The younger generation ________ a society is always distinguished ________ the older generation ________ number ________ ways. They dress and conduct themselves differently and also think differently. They attach a lot ________ importance ________ their external appearance. They try to be as attractive as possible and one sure way ________ being so is to try to adopt the latest fashions. It seems to be vital ________ young people to be fashionable; fashions refer ________ periodic changes ________ the habits ________ people, mainly ________ reference ________ the style of clothes and hair-do.

Conjunctions

Conjunctions are words that connect two words, phrases, clauses or sentences. For example,

John's brother *and* Mary's sister are my best friends.
I reached the station in time, *but* the train had already left.
I shall ring you up tonight *or* see you tomorrow morning.

She told me *that* she was too tired.

Unless it rains within the next few days, there will be a severe drought.

I reached the station *before* the train left.

Conjunctions like *and*, *but* and *or* establish a relationship of grammatical equality between the two units joined, whereas conjunctions like *that*, *if*, *unless* and *before* establish a relationship of grammatical inequality between the two units joined. Conjunctions of the first type may be referred to as co-ordinating conjunctions and those of the second type may be referred to as subordinating conjunctions.

Co-ordinating Conjunctions

The three basic co-ordinating conjunctions are *and*, *but* and *or*. The pair *both...and* is similar in meaning to *and* and the pairs *either...or* and *neither...nor* are similar to *or*.

The following are the basic meanings of the three co-ordinating conjunctions. Sentences are given to illustrate these meanings.

Uses of **and**

1. a sequence of events – She opened the door *and* went out.
2. effect – He touched the electric wire *and* got a mild shock.
3. contrast – He promised to help me *and* he disappeared from the scene.
4. comment – Everyone hated him for his tall claims about himself *and* that's not at all surprising.
5. condition – Ask him to speak *and* he will never stop.

Use of **but**

The most important use of *but* is to show contrast. For example,

The doctors did their best to save the patient, *but* they didn't succeed.

Uses of **or**

1. choice – You may have tea *or* coffee.
2. restatement – She is very happy, *or* she seems to be very happy.
3. negative condition – Start early *or* you will be late.

Subordinating Conjunctions

The subordinating conjunctions *if* and *unless* indicate conditions. *Unless* means *if...not* and refers to a negative condition. For example,

If you work hard, you will certainly succeed.

Unless you work hard, you will not be able to make good progress.

The subordinating conjunctions *though* and *although* introduce a contrast. For example,

Though/Although he watered the plants regularly, they did not grow well.

The subordinating conjunctions *when*, *while*, and *as* are used to express time. For example,

Mother was cooking *while* the children were playing in the garden.

The subordinating conjunctions *as*, *because* and *since* express the cause or reason of something. For example,

I was unable to write to you earlier, *as* I was busy with my assignments.

The subordinating conjunction *so that* introduces the purpose or intention in doing something.

He started early from home *so that* he could reach the hall in time.

Exercise D

Fill in the blanks in the following sentences, using appropriate conjunctions.

1. You can buy a green shirt ________ a blue shirt ________ both.
2. We were expected to file our nominations ________ then start talking to the delegates.
3. Television has opened up an altogether new world for us ________ at the same time it has given rise to a number of problems.
4. ________ I heard the explosion, I rushed out of the building.
5. ________ I had worked hard, I would have been much more successful in life.
6. Some people are really very unlucky. They work very hard ________ they never succeed.
7. Keep pressing the switch ________ I ask you to stop.
8. ________ the bell rang, the students rushed out of the class.
9. He thinks that he can talk rudely to me just ________ he is my boss.
10. This was reported in newspapers, ________ you must remember ________ everything printed in newspapers is not necessarily true.
11. The roads have been dug up ________ new telephone lines can be laid.
12. The batsman completely missed the ball ________ got out.
13. The books will be distributed only ________ all the formalities are completed.
14. He commented ________ the dress looked very nice.
15. ________ he is poor, he is very happy.

16. Cars have started using liquid petroleum gas as a fuel ________ it is much cheaper than petrol.

17. ________ he escaped unhurt is a great consolation.

18. We haven't met ________ you left Delhi .

19. It is a good indication ________ people are more and more conscious of health.

20. Try and try again ________ you succeed.

21. The British are supposed to be reserved ________ reticent, ____________ the Indians are generally described as warm ________ talkative.

22. I was keen on watching the serial on television, ________ there was no power supply at that time.

23. Exercise well every day ________ you will get fat.

24. _____ the weather had improved considerably, we decided to move on.

25. Try and try again ________ you will succeed.

26. I would like to know ________ the banks are open today.

27. I have never seen such a beautiful sight so far ________ I am not likely to see such a sight again.

28. I shall help you on one condition ________ that is ________ you will keep this confidental.

29. ________ he is a complete fool, he will be able to follow the lecture.

Simple, Compound and Complex Sentences

Grammar makes available to us a number of ways of expressing our meaning in order to achieve different effects. Sentences are divided into three types, depending on the construction of sentences in terms of clauses—simple, compound and complex.

Consider the following set of sentences.

a. I opened the door. I saw a ghost.
b. I opened the door and saw a ghost.
c. When I opened the door, I saw a ghost.

The three sets of sentences given above mean almost the same, but they are constructed differently. Sentence (a) is a sequence of two simple sentences, (b) is a compound sentence and (c) is a complex sentence.

As you know, a sentence consists of one or more finite clauses. A clause is a grammatical unit which necessarily has a verb phrase in it. The easiest way of finding out the number of clauses in a sentence is to count the number of verb phrases in it. The number of clauses is the same as the number of verb phrases in it. The following are examples of sentences having one, two, three and four clauses.

I have been playing cricket for the last ten years. – one clause

I have been playing cricket since I left school. – two clauses

He came, he saw and he conquered. – three clauses

I have been playing cricket since I left school and I shall continue with cricket till I retire from my job. – four clauses

A simple sentence consists of a single clause. That is, it has a single verb phrase in it. In example (a) given above, opened is the verb phrase in the first sentence and saw is a verb phrase in the second sentence. The following are a few more examples of simple sentences.

We are leaving tomorrow.
She has decided to study music.
Could you help me, please?
I expect you to work harder.

In example (b), 'and' is the co-ordinating conjunction used and the two clauses are seen as equal in rank. Co-ordinating conjunctions establish grammatical equality between two clauses. Such clauses are called co-ordinate clauses. A sentence which consists of two or more co-ordinate clauses is called a compound sentence.

The following are some more examples of compound sentences.

I reached the station in time, but the train had already left.
She touched the wire and got an electric shock.
Start early or you will be late.
The maid has washed and dried all the clothes.

In example (c) above 'when' is the subordinating conjunction used. A clause beginning with a subordinating conjuction is called a subordinate or dependent clause. The other clause, which can stand by itself, is called a principal or independent clause . In some sense, a subordinate clause is seen as lower in rank to the principal clause. Therefore, such a sentence is characterised by grammatical inequality of the two clauses. A sentence which consists of one principal clause and one or more subordinate clauses is called a complex sentence. The following are some more examples of complex sentences.

I was counting the forms when you entered the room.
We watered all the plants regularly so that they would grow well.
If you have any problem, you can consult the director.
We were late because there was a traffic jam.

Exercise E

Read the following sentences carefully and specify whether they are simple, compound or complex sentences.

1. Your report should contain all the information that is relevant to the subject matter.

2. Do you know that the wedding has been postponed?

3. The supplier did not honour my request for a replacement of the goods and lost a customer for ever.

4. I shall be grateful to you if I am invited for the interview.

5. Science has broken down the barriers of space and time.

6. The thing that a nation must protect itself from is internal rot.

7. You have to acquire a character which will raise the whole life of the people amidst whom you move and for whom you are expected to work.

8. A world authority to be effective must be based on a world understanding or world community.

9. Evil is whatever springs from weakness.

10. We are always doing something for posterity, but I would like to see posterity do something for us.

Subordinate clauses are divided into three types—noun clause, adjective clause and adverb clause. A noun clause performs the typical function of a noun phrase, that is, it functions as the subject, object or complement. Consider the following examples of noun clauses.

That he escaped unhurt is a great consolation.

She told me that the examinations were postponed.

The problem is that all the banks are closed today.

I think that we get the best kind of cloth in this shop.

An adjective clause performs the typical function of an adjective phrase, i.e. it gives us more information about a noun phrase. An adjective clause begins with the subordinating conjunction *who* (*whom/ whose*), *which* or *that*. Consider the following examples of adjective clauses.

The book which you want is not available in the library.

The man who is waiting outside is my best friend.

Delhi, which is the capital if India, is a big city.

My friend has recently bought a car which was imported from Japan.

An adverb clause performs the typical functions of an adverb phrase, i.e. to give information about circumstances in which an action is performed. Adverb clauses typically convey information about time, place and manner. They also express conditions, contrasts, reasons, purposes, effects etc.

The following are some examples of adverb clauses.

While I was waiting to see the doctor, I came across this advertisement in a magazine.

Unless it rains soon, there will be a drought.

He worked very hard so that he could complete all his assignments in time.

Althougth he was angry, he didn't say a word.

Exercise F

Identify subordinate clauses from the following sentences and say whether they are noun clauses, adjective clauses or adverb clauses.

1. The story that he told his wife is not true.
2. They supported me whenever I was in difficulty.
3. What you say is absolutely right.
4. The mechanic pointed out that all the electric wires had been disconnected.
5. Because you asked me to wait here, I didn't move from here.
6. Some people do not smile even if they are happy.
7. I am always available in case you need any help.
8. The student who answered that question is extremely intelligent.
9. Hyderabad, which is the capital of Andhra Pradesh, has many places worth visiting.
10. I am looking for someone who is an expert in mathematics.
11. She asked me whether I was married.
12. How you will make all the arrangements is not clear to me.
13. Try to persuade him to join the club, if you can.
14. I would like to complete all the formalities before we sign the documents.

In the rest of this unit, let us consider how to transform a sentence into another type without changing the meaning.

Conversion of a simple sentence into a complex sentence

When we convert a simple sentence into a complex sentence, we must use at least two clauses and one of them must begin with a subordinating conjunction. This can be done by expanding a phrase or non-finite clause into a finite clause. Here are some examples.

a. Simple – He pleaded total ignorance in the matter.
   Complex – He pleaded that he was totally ignorant in the matter.

b. Simple – Despite his protests, the management went on with its original plan.
   Complex – Though he protested, the management went on with its original plan.

c. Simple – This is not the way to introduce the chief guest .
   Complex – This is not the way in which we should introduce the chief guest.

d. Simple – To my shock, he left the hall without informing anyone.
   Complex – I was shocked that he left the hall without informing anyone.

e. Simple – Being rich, he is not bothered about the consequences of his actions.
   Complex – Because / As he is rich, he is not bothered about the consequences of his action.

Conversion of a complex sentence into a simple sentence

For converting a complex sentence into a simple sentence, we generally need to express the meaning of the subordinate clause using just a word or a phrase.

a. Complex – Wars should be avoided so that democracy succeeds.
   Simple – Wars should be avoided for the success of democracy.

b. Complex – I am responsible for whatever I decide.
   Simple – I am responsible for all my decisions.

c. Complex – The report that he behaved in an irresponsible manner shocked me.
   Simple – The report of his irresponsible behaviour shocked me.

d. Complex – Even if you are cautious, you might make some mistakes.
   Simple – Despite your caution you might make some mistakes.

e. Complex – I rushed out of the room when I heard the deafening sound of the explosion.
   Simple – I rushed out of the room on hearing the deafening sound of the explosion.

Conversion of a simple sentence into a compound sentence

For converting a simple sentence into a compound sentence, we should have at least two clauses joined by a co-ordinating conjunction like *and* or *but*.

a. Simple – In spite of his problems he completed the assignment in time.
   Compound – He had problems, but he completed the assignment in time./He had problems and still/(yet) he completed the assignment in time.

b. Simple – In addition to offering useful advice, the manager helped me in getting the job.
   Compound – The manager offered me useful advice and also helped me in getting the job.

c. Simple – On hearing the deafening sound of the explosion, I rushed out of the room.
   Compound – I heard the deafening sound of the explosion and I rushed out of the room.

Conversion of a compound sentence into a simple sentence

For converting a compound sentence into a simple sentence, we need to remove the co-ordinating conjunction and use only one clause.

a. Compound – He is a foreigner and yet he speaks Marathi well.
   Simple – In spite of being a foreigner, he speaks Marathi well.

b. Compound – You must study hard or you will not do well in the examinations.
   Simple – You must study hard in order to do well in the examinations.

Conversion of a complex sentence into a compound sentence

a. Complex – Though he was tired, he continued with his journey.
   Compound – He was tired and yet he continued with his journey.

b. Complex – If you do not co-operate with the investigating team, you will be dismissed from the job.
   Compound – Co-operate with the investigating team or you will be dismissed from the job.

c. Complex – People know very well that exercise is a must for a healthy body and mind.
   Compound – Exercise is a must for a healthy body and mind and people know that very well.

Conversion of a compound sentence into a complex sentence

a. Compound – He wanted to get married soon and registered himself at a marriage bureau.
   Complex – He registered himself at a marriage bureau because he wanted to get married soon.

b. Compound – I have tried to read this book several times, but I was never able to go beyond the first ten pages.
   Complex – Even though I have tried to read this book several times, I was never able to go beyond the first ten pages.

c. Compound – Attend the classes regularly or your terms will not be granted.

Complex – If you do not attend the classes regularly, your terms will not be granted.

Exercise G

Convert each of the following sentences into the type of sentence indicated in brackets.

1. Reach home in time or you will miss the most interesting television programme. (complex)
2. He has lost the books borrowed from the library. (complex)
3. We were so tired that we could not walk any longer. (simple)
4. Although they were defeated, they did not lose hope. (compound)
5. He cannot make any furniture now because all his tools are very old. (simple)
6. Everyone knows that we must use solar energy as an alternative source of energy. (compound)
7. He made many tall promises but disappeared from the scene at a critical moment. (simple)
8. He had no experience of teaching and he proved to be a failure as a teacher. (complex)
9. He had every qualification for the job except experience. (compound)
10. He shouted at the top of his voice. (complex)

REVISION

In this unit, we shall revise some of the grammar topics studied earlier. You will find here a reminder of some of the rules that you already know, a few examples and some exercises.

Tenses

We need to be particularly careful in the use of the following tenses—present perfect, present perfect progressive and past perfect. Using tenses correctly in sequences, i.e. in connected pieces of discourse, is a challenging task. It is useful to know the contrast between tenses. Consider the following pairs of sentences.

a. He is working on the assignment.

b. He has worked on the assignment.

Sentence (a) indicates that his work on the assignment is incomplete, whereas (b) indicates that it is already completed .

a. I have lived in Pune for twenty years.

b. I have been living in Pune for twenty years.

Sentence (a) is ambiguous, because it does not tell us clearly whether the person lives in Pune at present. It only says that so far (i.e. in the past) he spent twenty years in Pune. He may or may not be living in Pune at present. Sentence (b) clearly indicates that the person has lived in Pune for the last twenty years and that he is still living there.

a. I read the book in 1990.

b. I have read this book.

When a specific time like 'in 1990' is mentioned, we use the simple past tense, but when it is not mentioned, we use the present perfect tense. The present perfect tense relates a past action to the present. Sentence (b) may imply the meaning 'I know what this book is about' or 'I still remember what I read.'

We should also remember the difference between stative and dynamic verbs. Stative verbs cannot generally be used in the progressive aspect. They are verbs like *be*, *seem*, *know*, *believe*, *understand*, *have* (possess), *consist*, *belong* and *own*.

Exercise A

Use the correct tense forms of the verbs given in brackets to complete the following sentences. Remember that in some cases, two or more answers are possible.

1. John (not know) that we (get) all the books on this subject issued from the library.

2. I (play) cricket for ten years. But I (have) to give it up when the doctors (advise) me against it after I (get) injured in an accident. However, even now I (derive) a lot of pleasure from cricket. I (not miss) the live telecast of any cricket match on television.

3. I (think) that in view of the rising prices of diesel and petrol we (have) to depend on solar energy more and more. A wonderful thing about it (be) that it never (get) exhausted. Moreover, I (believe) it (not cause) much pollution.

4. On her arrival in India on 29 June, Sheila (tell) me that she (study) French for ten years and that she (plan) to do research in French. Then she (add) that she (like) to translate a French novel into English after she (complete) her Ph.D.

5. When Father (return) home in the evening, children (play) hide and seek. Before this they (finish) playing indoor games like cards and chess. But now it (be) time for them to go out in the open. They (like) to play cricket every evening.

Conditional Sentences

Conditional sentences are sentences using 'if' or 'unless'. There are four patterns of the use of tenses in conditional sentences.

Pattern I	Present + present *If you heat a metal, it expands.*
Pattern II	Present + future *If the match is over early, the players will leave for Delhi by the evening flight.*
Pattern III	Simple past + would +v *If I won a lottery prize, I would buy a car.*
Pattern IV	Past perfect + would + have + v +en *If I had known about the consequences of smoking, I would have given it up long ago.*

Exercise B

1. *In the following exercise, the conditional clauses are given Complete the sentence using an appropriate principal clause. Pay attention to the sequence of tenses.*

1. If I had joined the course in time, ____________________
2. If I need some postage stamps, ____________________
3. If I were you, ____________________
4. If there were no computers, ____________________
5. If I become the Prime Minister of India, ____________________
6. If I were on the moon now, ____________________
7. If you exercise, ____________________
8. If you want to improve your vocabulary, ____________________
9. If you children are hungry now, ____________________
10. Unless it rains this year, ____________________

2. *In the following conditional sentences, the principal clauses are given. Supply an appropriate conditional clause.*

1. I would have published my book of poetry, if ______________
2. I don't mind coming to your house, if ___________________
3. I won't be able to see you for quite some time unless _________
4. I would not tolerate such a remark, if ___________________
5. I will have to rewrite the draft of the letter, if ______________

The Passive Voice

The passive voice is generally used when the agent or doer of the action is unimportant because it is very general (e.g. *people*, *they* and *someone*) or because it can be easily guessed from the context. For example,

Some of the luggage has been stolen from the cloak-room.

It is generally believed in the west that 13 is an unlucky number.

Exercise C

Change the following into the passive voice.

1. Someone has changed the computer entries during my absence.
2. Seal the packet here.
3. In order to open the bottle, you should heat the top portion of the bottle and then you should gently pull off the seal.
4. Has the secretary of the class distributed the handouts?
5. One should file the income tax returns by 30 June every year.
6. The storm destroyed 200 houses in the coastal areas.

7. Students may pay the fees in three instalments. They should pay the first instalment before the commencement of the course. They can pay the second instalment in the second or third month of the course. They must pay the final instalment before the examination.

8. The authors wrote the book under great pressure of time.

9. The mechanic has already restored the telephone connection.

10. We had to invite an expert from Mumbai to repair the machine.

Reported Speech

You already know that in direct speech , we give the speaker's exact words, whereas in indirect or reported speech, we report in our own words what the speaker said. If the reporting verb (e.g. asked, ordered, pointed out and commented) is in the past tense, the present tense of the direct speech changes into the past tense. Similarly, there are appropriate changes in demonstratives (e.g. this–that) and adverbials (e.g. now–then).

Exercise D

Change the following into reported speech.

1. Mr. Joshi asked at the counter, 'Where can I buy a copy of the latest railway time-table?' The man at the counter said, 'From the next shop.'

2. Clerk: May I know your name, please?
Ravi: Ravi Jagdale.
Clerk: How long do you propose to stay here?
Ravi: For about a week.
Clerk: Do you want to have a single room or a double room?
Ravi: I would certainly prefer a single room. What are the charges for a single room?
Clerk: Rs. 350/- per day.
Ravi: Do I have to pay any advance?
Clark: Just one day's charges.
Ravi: Here you are.
Clerk: Thank you. I'll give you a receipt.

Modal Auxiliaries

Verbs like 'can', 'may', 'might', 'should' and 'will' are called modal auxiliary verbs. Each modal auxiliary verb is associated with a number of meanings and you should be particular about the correct use of these verbs.

Exercise E

1. Distinguish between the following pairs of sentences.

1. i. It may rain tomorrow.
   ii. It might rain tomorrow.

2. i. You must not carry an umbrella with you.
   ii. You need not carry an umbrella with you.

3. i. You should obey your parents.
   ii. You have to obey your parents

4. i. Shall I leave early tomorrow?
   ii. Should I leave early tomorrow?

2. Fill in the blanks in the following sentences, using appropriate auxiliary verbs.

1. The teacher said to the students, 'You ________ refer to my personal books for writing the essay.'

2. The deadline for submitting the assignment is tomorrow. I ________ work throughout the night in order to complete it.

3. ________ you please explain how I ________ reach this address?

4. How ________ you take the class for a swim when half of them don't know swimming?

5. You ________ to study harder in order to surpass your classmates.

Punctuation

Usually we do not attach much importance to punctuation marks. But correct punctuation is a great help to the reader and it indicates how careful the writer is. Sometimes, a change of punctuation can bring about a change in the meaning or function of a sentence. Consider the following sentences carefully.

a. i. How beautiful the picture is!
   ii. How beautiful is the picture?

b. i. 'Inspector,' said the woman, 'has been chasing the burglars.'
   ii. Inspector said, 'The woman has been chasing the burglars.'

c. i. The vehicles were moving slowly. The policeman asked them to move on.
   ii. The vehicles were moving. Slowly, the policeman asked them to move on.

Exercise F

Punctuate the following sentences.

1. oh my god said the poor man im completely ruined
2. have you ever got lost in london said the foreigner no never said the manager
3. would you mind said the guest passing the salt please
4. i would like to have the following things from the market some paper a writing pad some new pens and some clips
5. wonderful your performance has just been superb applauded the visitors
6. johns uncle is a very strict disciplinarian isnt he
7. im extremely sorry to have missed your lecture said the student never mind said the teacher
8. where can i buy the latest railway time table asked the customer over there replied the man at the counter
9. whats your good name asked the indian host i dont have a good name or a bad name i just have a name replied the british visitor
10. wish you good luck

Reference Skills

Introduction

To be able to communicate effectively it is necessary to have proficiency in language skills—namely listening, speaking, reading, and writing. In addition to language skills you should also know reference skills.

'To refer to' means 'to look for' or 'to try to find out a piece of information that one needs'. If we fail to understand something vital while reading something or watching a TV programme or listening to someone, we need to make use of the relevant reference material. When you want to prepare a speech, make a presentation or give a demonstration you may have to make sure that the information given is correct and therefore you have to confirm it. You are likely to participate in seminars, workshops, group discussions and before you do so you have got to know about the subject to be talked about and you must get information about it from the appropriate sources. When you read about the subject of your study you are likely to come across a number of words which you do not know. Unless you look up such words in a dictionary you will not understand the matter you are reading. Therefore, to possess the ability to find out the required information from the concerned source is to be able to add to your fund of knowledge and promote your intellectual growth. Before you go in search of any piece of information,

a. You should know different sources of reference materials available.
b. You should be able to acquire or locate the reference materials.
c. You should be able to look up the reference you want.

For example, if you want information about a flowering plant 'dahlia' you should know that the dictionary of gardening exists. Then you should be able to know where that dictionary would be available. When it is made available you should be able to look up the item 'dahlia'.

Now we will find out how information is looked up in reference materials.

Looking up the Dictionary

Various types of dictionaries available in the market are as follows:

a. **A bilingual dictionary**: This dictionary gives us meanings of words in English as well as in one of the languages other than English—for example, Marathi and Hindi. If you wish to get the meaning in your mother tongue, then go for the bilingual dictionary that gives meanings in your mother tongue as well as English. This dictionary is good at the school level. It is also useful when you wish to have the exact equivalence of a word in Marathi.

b. **A monolingual or English–English dictionary**: This dictionary gives information about the vocabulary items only in English. If you are studying a particular subject only through English then it is better to use this kind of a dictionary. Such a dictionary at the advanced level deals with vocabulary items from the point of view of usage and provides illustrations of contextual use of words. Some dictionaries, on the other hand, give, apart from meanings, the etymological information about the word. One such dictionary is Chambers dictionary.

c. **A picture dictionary**: This dictionary gives pictures of objects and lables them or their parts. Most of the dictionaries do have pictures that are essential but a picture dictionary gives only pictures and indicates meanings.

d. **An encyclopedic dictionary**: This dictionary includes items which usually are not found in the ordinary dictionaries. For example, the items Andaman Nicobar' will not be recorded in the usual dictionaries but its information in a broad way would be found in the encyclopedic dictionary. The Random House Dictionary of the English Language is a dictionary of this sort.

e. **An English–Marathi/Hindi dictionary**: This is also a bilingual dictionary which gives meanings in only one language such as Marathi or Hindi and so on. If you want the meanings only in your mother tongue then you should use this kind of a dictionary.

Subject-wise dictionaries are available. Take a look at some of the following dictionaries. Each of these dictionaries explains the items of the subject it deals with.

- Dictionary of Philosophy.
- Dictionary of Architecture.
- Dictionary of Linguistics.
- Dictionary of Literary terms.
- Dictionary of Commerce.
- Dictionary of Legal terms.

The structure of a dictionary is as follows:

a. In the beginning it gives information about the dictionary and how to look it up.
b. It lists the entries in the alphabetical order.
c. Various appendices i.e. sections that give extra information are at the end of the dictionary. For example, the appendix of chemical elements, irregular verbs, punctuation, writing and so on.

Usually the dictionary gives information about the items as follows:

a. Spelling and its variations: for example–color (American)
colour (English)

b. Pronunciation: It may be in a phonetic script. For example education /edjʊˈkeɪʃən/ or it may have used its own symbols. Whatever the case the key is given on the coverpage, initially or at the end. Some dictionaries give alternative pronunciation. The stressed syllable is indicated by a short vertical bar placed above and before the first letter of the stressed syllable. This means the unit with the stress mark (ˈ) is to be spoken comparatively with a greater breath force.

c. Grammatical information about the item: For example–educate (v), education (n), educational (adj)

d. Various meanings: For example, head–a part of our body, the head of a nail, the head of a tape recorder, the head of an organisation, etc.

e. Various words made from it with their meanings: head, headless, headline, headlight, headphones, headquarters, etc.

f. Phrases made from the items and their meanings: to keep one's head, to loose one's head, to use one's head, to make head or tail of something, to put your/our/ their heads together, etc.

Here is a list of some useful dictionaries.

1. A Dictionary of Social Sciences, Hugo F Reading 1977 Ambika Publication, New Delhi.

2. A Dictionary of Sociology, (ed) G Duncan Mitchell, 1968 Routledge & Kegan Poul, London.

3. A Dictionary of Printing & Publishing, P H Collin, 1989, Peter Collin Publishing Ltd, Middlesex.

4. A Dictionary of Environment, Gurdeep Raj, 1986, Anmol Publication, New Delhi.

5. A Dictionary of Economics & Commerce, J A Hanson 1965 Mac Donald's Evans Plymouth Ltd.

6. A Dictionary of Geography, W G Moose 1968. Penguin.

7. The Penguin Dictionary of Architecture, John Fleming et al 1966.

8. A Dictionary of Art & Artists, 1968 Penguin.

9. A Dictionary of Anthropology, E B Tylor, 1991 Goyl Saab, Delhi.

10. A Dictionary of Information Technology, (ed) Kapoor & Gupta 1995, Amit Atwal, Delhi.

Exercise A

Find out various meanings of the following words from a good dictionary.

board	book	ground	run	cut	net

Finding out References

Suppose you want to find out the term 'leg break' related to cricket, go to the cupboard where books of sports are placed. Get a book on cricket. For example, *How to Play Cricket* by Ian Morrison, 1990, Ward Lock Limited, London. Under 'Equipment and Terminology' on page 28 you will get information about the term as follows:

Leg break : A ball that moves from leg to off after pitching.

You will also see the diagram as given below :

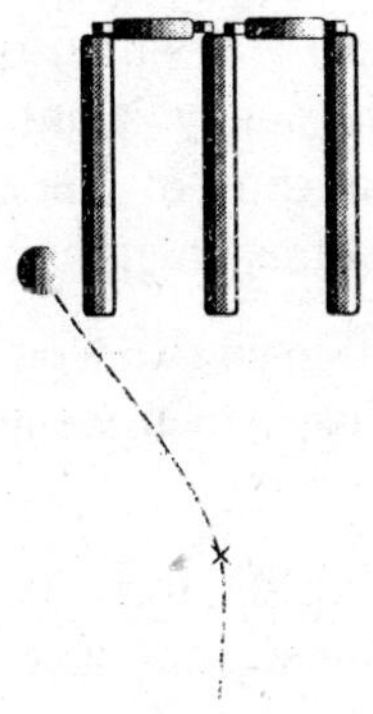

Leg Break

A ball that moves from leg to off after pitching at 'x' is a leg break.

You will get information about a number of terms–like 'inswinger', 'full toss', 'night watchman', 'yorker', 'glance', 'hook', 'cut', and so on. If you want to know about hockey, go to Gian Singh's *The Hockey Book*, 1982. Orient Paper back.

You can also get answers to the questions such as:

a. 'What is the duration of the hockey game?' (p. 117) or

b. 'What is the length of the hockey stick?' (p. 129).

You will find answers as follows:

a. The match shall consist of the regular duration of two periods of 35 minutes each separated by an interval which shall not exceed 10 minutes. (minimum 5 minutes)

b. Not specified in the rules. It depends on the suitability of a player.

If you want to know about 'black belt' from karate, get a book like *Step by Step Karate Skills* by Don Bradely 1987 the Hamlyn Publishing Group Limited London and you will find it on page 125. You will also find a list of Japanese words most commonly used in karate on page 124 such as 'yokogeri', 'side kick', 'oi zuki', 'lunse punch', 'sensei teacher', 'shihan master', and so on. If you want to acquaint yourself with the term 'pranayama' you have a book on yoga such as *Light on Pranayama* by BKS Iyengar 1992, Harper Collins Publishers, London and on page 278 the term is defined as 'rhythmic control of breath'. You will also get the information about the propounder of Yoga philosophy Patanjali, the author of *Yoga Sutra* who is also a reputed author of the *Mahabhasya*, the great commentary on Panini's Sutras on grammar.

Thus you can have information you want on gymnastics, chess, cycling, boxing, wrestling, football, basketball, weightlifting, rugby, badminton, billiards, tennis and so on.

Many students do not have a dictionary which is always required in day-to-day life. Some of those who have a dictionary do not know how to refer to it. Many people are often lazy in looking for references. If you are unable to find out the required references you may feel handicapped.

Apart from various dictionaries information is available in encyclopedias, year-books, books of records, who's who books etc. If you are interested in knowing about extinct animals, for example, go to page 64 of *Oxford Childrens Pocket Book of Facts*, and you will come to know that 99% of the animal species that ever lived are now extinct. *Beacon's Junior Encyclopaedia*, Hui Edition, 1995 offers useful and interesting information about our universe, planets, geology, geography, medicine, sports, and so on.

A Thesaurus is another important treasure of information about words, their synonyms and antonyms. I. A. Richards, in the introduction to *Roget's Pocket Thesaurus* says:

'A Thesaurus is the opposite of a dictionary. You turn to the Thesaurus when you know the meaning already but don't yet have the word. It may be on the tip of your tongue, but what it is you don't yet know. It is like the missing piece of a puzzle. You know well enough that the other words you try out won't do. They say too much or too little. They haven't the punch or have too much. They are too flat or too showy, too kind or too cruel. But the word which just fills the bill won't come, so you reach for the Thesaurus.'

Suppose you want to describe the Taj Mahal you saw on a moonlit night. You say, 'In the moon light the Taj Mahal looked extremely beautiful.'

You feel that the expression 'extremely beautiful' does not describe what you have seen. So, you replace it by 'marvellous' and you are not still happy about the word. You refer to the entry 'beautiful' in a Thesaurus and you get the following list:

> beautiful, beauteous, handsome, pretty, lovely, graceful, elegant, exquisite, delicate, dainty, comely, fair, goodly, bonny, good-looking, well favoured, well formed, well proportioned, shapely, symmetrical, harmonious, bright, bright-eyed, rosy-cheeked, rosy, ruddy, blooming, in full bloom

You can also find words like:

> marvellous, splendid, majestic, wonderful, charming, attractive, fascinating, tempting, appealing, inviting, challenging, sensuous, sensual, sensational, exciting, amazing, shocking, killing

Though all these words appear to be similar they are used differently in different contexts and they express various shades of meaning. In the above example you are most likely to say,

> 'In the moon light the Taj Mahal looked splendid.'

because the word 'splendid' implies the grandeur, elegance and impressiveness of the Taj.

A Thesaurus also gives antonyms. For example, for 'ugly' which is the opposite of the word 'beautiful', you will find a number of words. Thesauruses are helpful for improving one's vocabulary.

Even newspapers and magazines can offer a lot of information. Reading newspapers daily and magazines regularly keeps you informed on a variety of topics such as — education, politics, population, social problems, national issues, environmental problems, health problems and so on.

Read the letter given below published in one of the issues of *The Indian Express*.

> *Why was Bombay renamed as Mumbai?*
>
> In the Marathi language, Bombay has been referred to as Mumbai for more than 200 years. But it has not always been so. Mumbai has an ancient temple dedicated to Mumbadevi. The real name of this deity was Maha Amba Devi or Maha Amba Ayi (Mother).
>
> Maha Amba Ayi got corrupted to Maha Ambayi, then to Mambayi and finally to Mumbai. According to *Murray's Handbook*, the name is possibly derived from Mumba Bai, the word used by the local kolis for the goddess. The Portuguese think the word 'Bombay' is derived from the Portuguese words — Bom Bahia or Fair Bay.

Using Table of Contents and Indexes to Locate Information

A table of contents is a list of items arranged in a sequential manner. It is given in the beginning of a book. It tells you about

i. What a book contains, and

ii. On which page a particular topic is. The number of pages devoted to each topic can give one a rough idea as to what extent the topic has been dealt with. Once you know the contents, you can go to a particular page for a particular topic you are interested in.

In fact you should know how to 'browse through' a book. When you come across a new book of any sort you should take into account the following:

a. First note the tittle of the book and the writer(s) name on the cover page which give you a general idea of what the book is about. For example, the title, *The Children's Treasury of Knowledge Underwater Life*, distributed by Time-Life Books tells us that the book is about under-water life and it is meant for mainly children (though it can always be useful to students of any age.)

b. Usually, at the back of the cover page or a page after but invariably on the left side page the following information about the book is given.

   i. The year of publication: You should pay attention to this because this will enable you to get the latest book in the given subject. For example,

> ORIENT LONGMAN LIMITED
>
> *Registerd Office*
> 3-6-272 Himayatnagar, Hyderabad 500 029 (A.P.). India
>
> *Other Offices*
> Bangalore/Bhopal/Bhubaneshwar/Calcutta/Chandigarh
> Chennai/Ernakulam/Guwahati/Hyderabad/Jaipur
> Lucknow/Mumbai/New Delhi/Patna
>
> © University of Pune 1999
>
> ISBN 81 250 1723 2
>
> *Typeset in Aldine by*
> OSDATA, Hyderabad 500 029
>
> *Printed in India at*
> SG Printers, Mumbai 400 011
>
> *Published by*
> Orient Longman Limited
> 3-5-820, Hyderguda
> Hyderabad 500 029

ii. The edition: It is 'a form in which a book is published'. For example, a paperback edition, hardback/bound edition, or de luxe edition.

You should look for the latest edition, if there is any, of the book you are looking for because normally in a new edition necessary revisions and useful additions are made and outdated information is deleted. The 'new edition' or 'the revised edition' is an improved version of the earlier one.

Sometimes the same book is just reprinted without any alterations. A book of this kind is called a 'reprint' or an 'impression'. The reprint or the impression can also be first, second or third and so on. For example, Wren and Martin's *High School Grammar and Composition* originally published in the 1930's and later on revised by N D V Prasadarao has run into many editions. There have been many impressions during the period 1973–99 which means this book has been reprinted many times in its present edition. This shows the popularity of the book.

c. The table of contents or index: As has already been pointed out,. this is a mirror to the whole book. Look at the following example from the book. *A Theory of Linguistic sign:*

CONTENTS

Source: *A Theory of Linguistic Sign* by Keller Rudi, 1995 OUP

d. The 'preface', 'foreword' or 'introduction': It is always helpful to go through the preface since it quickly and precisely gives the idea about the subject area of the book, the purpose for which the book has been written, the target readers and the general presentation of the book. Thus, it tells in a nut-shell what the book is about. Read the 'foreword' of Raja Rao to his famous novel *Kanthapura*.

FOREWORD

My publishers have asked me to say a word of explanation.

There is no village in India, however mean, that has not a rich sthala-purana, *or legendary history, of its own. Some god or godlike hero has passed by the village—Rama might have rested under this pipal-tree, Sita might have dried her clothes, after her bath, on this yellow stone, or the Mahatma himself, on one of his many pilgrimages through the country, might have slept in this hut, the low one, by the village gate. In this way the past mingles with the present, and the gods mingle with men to make the repertory of your grandmother always bright. One such story from the contemporary annals of my village I have tried to tell.*

The telling has not been easy. One has to convey in a language that is not one's own the spirit that is one's own. One has to convey the various shades and omissions of a certain thought-movement that looks maltreated in an alien language. I use the word 'alien', yet English is not really an alien language to us. It is the language of our intellectual make-up—like Sanskrit or Persian was before—but not of our emotional make-up. We are all instinctively bilingual, many of us writing in our own language and in English. We cannot write like the English. We should not. We cannot write only as Indians. We have grown to look at the large world as part of us. Our method of expression therefore has to be a dialect which will some day prove to be as distinctive and colourful as the Irish or the American. Time alone will justify it.

After language the next problem is that of style. The tempo of Indian life must be infused into our English expression, even as the tempo of American or Irish life has gone into the making of theirs. We, in India, think quickly, we talk quickly, and where we move we move quickly. There must be something in the sun of India that makes us rush and tumble and run on. And our paths are paths interminable. The Mahabharatha *has 214,778 verses and the* Ramayana *48,000. Puranas there are endless and innumerable. We have neither punctuation nor the treacherous 'ats' and 'ons' to bother us—we tell one interminable tale. Episode follows episode, and when our thoughts stop our breath stops, and we move on to another thought. This was and still is the ordinary style of our story-telling. I have tried to follow it myself in this story.*

It may have been told of an evening, when as the dusk falls and through the sudden quiet, lights leap up in house after house, and stretching her bedding on the veranda, a grandmother might have told you, newcomer, the sad tale of her village.

RAJA RAO

Source: *Kanthapura* 1971 Orient Paperback, Delhi

e. On the last page you are likely to get

i. general information about the book and

ii. information about the writer and

iii. extracts of the reviews about the book.

This information is very useful since it gives a general impression about the book. Look at the following back page of the book *Wole Soyinka: A Quest for Renewal* written by Mary T. David.

This up-to-date study of Wole Soyinka, Africa's Nobel Laureate, covers the entire range of his writing. The plays, poems, fiction, autobiographical pieces, literary criticism and polemical essays are subjected to a critical analysis that has as its focus his recurrent use of the theme of regeneration. Mary T. David resorts to a close reading of the texts and intertexts to show how the archetype for renewal persists in Soyinka's works in myriad forms, but mainly projected through myths and symbols of diverse provenance, such as Yoruba ontology, Judaeo-Christianity and European Literature. The resulting interpretation of the works is highly original and revealing. She sheds new light on Soyinka's art, arguing that his aesthetics and his social vision are both determined by his deep concern for renewal.

. . . .

Mary T. David lived in Nigeria for many years, teaching in the University of life. This has given her an abiding love of Africa and a deep understanding of Yoruba culture and society. She has lectured in reputed Universities in India and abroad and authored several books among which is *A History of American Literature*. Her interests include writing for children and translation. She has translated Mortimer Wheeler's *Archaeology from the Earth*, into Malayalam.

Mary David now lives in Kodaikanal working as Professor of English, Mother Teresa Women's University.

Cover design and illustration by Sunil Kishen

Source: *Wole Soyinka: A Quest for Renewal* by M T David 1995 B I Publications

f. The subject index: It is a list of items or topics which have been dealt with in the book. The index is usually found at the end of a book in the alphabetical order. The index helps us to look up the specific piece of information that has not been mentioned in the contents which includes only the broad topics.

Suppose you want to read the matter related to 'volcanoes' in a book of geology, 'stone age' in a book of history, 'diseases' in a book of medicine, 'atheletics' in a book of sports, 'classical music' in a book of music, 'super computer' in a book of computers, 'Indian Constitution' in a book of politics, 'Industrial Revolution', in a book of economics, 'stimulus' in a book of psychology, 'monogamy' in a book of sociology, 'feminist criticism' in a book related to literary criticism, or any item of this sort in an encyclopedia you do not have to turn the pages of the book. Instead, look for the entry with the same name in the index and go to the page immediately where it is discussed. This saves a lot of time. Just as looking up a word in a dictionary is a skill, referring to the index of a book and getting to the entry one wants in the shortest possible time is also an important skill. As a student you have to refer to a number of books for a particular topic, therefore, you must acquire this skill. You can look up the same item in different books and get more information about it. You can also compare how the same topic is treated by different authors differently.

g. An appendix is a section of a book that gives extra information at the end of a book. For example, the *Advanced Learner's Dictionary* (OUP) has several useful appendices, such as (1) Irregular verbs (2) Numbers (3) Punctuation and writing (4) Family relationships (5) Common first names (6) Ranks in the Armed Forces (7) Chemical elements (8) Notes on usage (9) Defining vocabulary.

It is interesting to study appendices. They increase our general knowledge.

Information Technology

The term 'Information Technology' (IT) refers to the use of electronic equipment, especially computers, for storing, analysing and distributing information of all kinds, including words, numbers and pictures. Previously, apart from written documents, information could be recorded in the form of audio and audio-visual cassettes, but with the advent of computer technology and mass communication we have found ourselves in the vast ocean of infinite information of multiple dimensions. A computer is like an 'Alladin's Lamp', which is ready to serve you every moment and produce any piece of information through internet at the press of a button. You can collect any amount of information on any subject from a variety of websites available on almost everything under the sun and even beyond; retain the obtained information as long as you want and utilise it according to your convenience. Right from multimedia, which involves several different methods of communication and forms of expression to virtual reality, which is a system in which images that look like real objects are created by the computer and appear to surround a person wearing special equipment, information is by our side, very close, press of a button away.

Obtaining information is no problem. The problem is to know the new ways and means of information and how to make use of it strategically. In future, they say, it is only those countries who have information and know how to use it cleverly will rule the world. Information is your strength. However, it will not come to you automatically. You must gain access to information. You should be able to access information; that is you should be able to open a computer file in order to get information from or put information into it or update the information already stored. You should be able to retrieve information, protect database, do data processing and use information appropriately. For this you need not be a computer engineer or computer expert but you have got to know computing, that is, you should know various computer operations. You should also learn to use computer operated articles like a calculator, an electronic diary and so on.

Libraries have also been computerised nowadays. Unless you know how to operate a computer, information will not be accessible to you. To be able to operate and use a computer is an inevitable reference skill.

The following interview published in *The Times of India*, highlights the significance of Information Technology in human life.

Better information, better health

MUMBAI: Considered an international leader in medical informatics with a special interest in electronic patient record systems, standards, networking and telemedicine, *C.Peter Waegemann*, executive director of the Medical Records Institute, a Boston-based organisation was in the city to educate medical professionals about the double revolution taking place in the health care sector—the empowerment of the patient via the Net and computers and connectivity. He spoke to *Amrita Nair-Ghaswalla* about the need to harness the fruits of the revolution for better patient care.

What exactly is an electronic patient record and why is it necessary to adopt the same in India?

Health is every person's greatest asset. The information regarding one's health consists of past medical record information including diagnoses, medications, allergies, surgeries, infections and other data. For most people this information in unique to the caregiver (read doctor). Over a period of time, however, this results in scattered pieces of health history that are often unrecoverable and irreconcilable. In the past, patient information was used only by the doctor. Now, as societies are moving from a paternalistic health care system, where the patient relies completely on the authoritarian role of the doctor, to a system of open partnership between health care providers and patients, health information needs to be made easily accessible, monitored and maintained even by patients. And with computerisation radically altering many areas of life and many workplace environments, the health care scene too has come under the spotlight. From the small office physician to the largest metropolitan hospital, the electronic health record system is changing the way we provide care. And since this is a new set of tools, which is changing the way medicine is being practised all over the world, it is time India too wakes up to the call.

How has the empowerment of the patient, with access to health information and services via the Internet, changed the scenario for doctors and health care providers?

For years, medical informatics professionals have been talking about 'patient-centered systems.' The Internet has made patient-centered health care systems possible now. Patients want to be involved in their health decisions, they want access to health information, to know about alternatives and are looking for efficiency and effectiveness.

Throughout the advanced and developing world the cry is going out, 'Better Infôrmation – Better Health'. This process is drastically changing the way that health caregivers work. Patients are seeking access to global health information from sources outside their traditional care delivery systems with the Internet facilitating these functions. This has enabled telecare service.

The Net is changing health care, leading to less encounters with the doctors. Satisfaction is taking priority, leading to different caregiver functions. Expectations of patients too are different. By becoming a privileged part of a global health care information network, doctors and health care providers will have to fully adapt to the new information age.

What exactly is ehealth?

Ehealth is a new term, characterising a wide range of health care changes, most of them enabled through the Internet. Through new technologies, patients are enabled to become partners in health care. This will have a tremendous impact on public health, patient encounters, caregivers' processes, health care cost reductions, and the quality of health care.

Ehealth brings to the fore connectivity where patients will be connected to caregivers through email and providers will provide new ways for telemedicine and telecare. With thousands of consumer health sites springing up providing valuable health information, millions of individuals are cruising the Web for 'second' opinions on all aspects of health care. There are online pharmacies, and Internet pharmacy services will increase as services will become more safe and reliable. The convenience and cost savings will make this an important field.

Moreover, as patients take charge of their health, the will want to have access to their health records. Internet-based personal health records are currently available from almost 30 companies. It should only be a matter of time before similar systems are in place in a country like India.

Source: *The Times of India*

Exercise B

1. *The following words have different connotations in the context of computer science. Refer to a dictionary of computing or a dictionary of multimedia, look them up and note down their meaning(s).*

memory	mouse	mail	chip	bug
character	bit	virus	graphics	storing

2. *Consult an encyclopedia and understand the following words/ phrases:*

phoenix	unicorn	Helen of Troy	Mona Lisa	dragon

3. *Study the phonetic symbols to know pronunciation better and learn to look up an English pronouncing dictionary from your teacher. Check up the pronunciation of the following words.*

paradise	disease	economics	increase	cosmetics
preface	breakfast	original	paralysis	petrol

4. *Visit your college library. Seek help from the librarian and teachers to locate the necessary reference materials to get information on the following.*

Mt. Vesuvius	bird migration	snakes	Diamond ring event
Honolulu			

5. *Collect as much, latest information as you can from various sources on the following:*

Kargil	Antartica	economic sanctions	our universe
Indian Writers in English		flying saucers and extraterrestrial life	

6. *Imagine that your younger brother/sister wants to be a pilot/marine biologist. (S)he expects you to guide him/her.*

   How will you go about collecting information about these professions? What information will you look for?

7. *Your friend is working on 'sugar factories'. One fine morning he realises that he needs a word for the topmost part of the sugar cane which consists of leaves and a flowery stem. He requests you to help him.*

   In what way would you help him getting the term?

8. *How will you make use of your knowledge about reference skills to understand the following passage.*

   The Internet can be described using several kinds of theories. Computer scientists have a variety of technical models of the Internet, these largely describe the mechanisms which facilitate communication, they don't aid in understanding how and why communication happens on the Internet. For us the theories about communication prove most useful in understanding tools and interactions in cyberspace.

9. *Let us imagine that you have heard a lot about Gang Tok/ Kanyakumari/Kulu Manali/Darjiling/Chandigarh/Mysore. You wish to visit the place. Mention various ways of getting information about it. For example, various ways of reaching the place, modes of travelling available, staying arrangements etc.*

   Write down the information you obtain.

INFORMATION TRANSFER

Introduction

Information can be presented in different ways depending on the demand of the situation. For example, information displayed in a tabular form in a college principal's office helps every visitor to quickly get an idea about the facultywise strength of students and teachers. Graphs and charts in books and magazines contain a lot of condensed information in a visible form and a reader, just at a glance, can draw comparisons and contrast and evaluate the situation depicted in them.

Information which is available in the verbal form can always be presented in the tabular or graphic form depending on the needs. Read the following information about the teaching staff of a college.

- The total teaching staff of the college is 300 of which one sixth, i.e. 52 are women teachers.
- The teachers who have obtained higher qualifications, i.e. higher than their post graduation are very few. They constitute just 20% of the total staff. Among them 15 teachers have qualified themselves for the M.Phil degree and 10 for the Ph.D. degree.
- A majority of teachers are permanent and their number is 238. The rest of the teachers are appointed on a temporary basis.
- As far as the age is concerned about half of the teachers are middle aged i.e. between 31 to 45 years. The number of younger teachers i.e. those between 25 to 30 and older ones, i.e. those above 45 is approximately the same. They are 73 and 77 respectively.

If the same information is put in the tabular form it is easy to read, understand and remember, and the time required to do this is much less than the time required to go through the information given in the above passage.

Look at the following table:

Teaching staff of the college–Total staff: 300

Sex		Qualifications			Appointment		Age group		
Male	Female	Post graduation	M.Phil	Ph.D	Temporary	Permanent	25-30	31-45	Above 45
248	52	275	15	10	62	238	73	150	77

The information given in the tabular form above can also be presented in the form of a tree diagram as shown below.

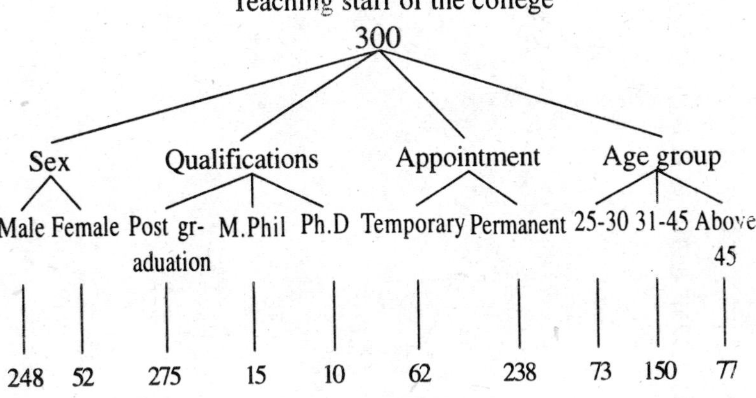

When the information is communicated through tables, charts and graphs, you should be able to interpret or analyse it and make observations about it. For example, one of the piece of information given is about the age group of the staff. The number of teachers between 31 to 45 is 150 and we can instantly draw a conclusion that half the teachers are middle aged. In terms of percentage the number is 50%. The number of teachers between 25 and 30 is 73 and of those above 45 is more or less the same. The numbers 73 as well as 77 are close to one fourth of the total. So the generalisation could be that the younger and older teachers are one fourth each of the total, which is 25%. This also means the number of the middle aged teachers is double the number of younger or older teachers.

Exercise A

Interpret the chart on page 66 and make observations about it.

DISTRIBUTION OF WORLD POPULATION

1950
2.52 Billion
More
Developed

0.50
6.50
8.70
10.60
6.60
12.00
28.40
26.70

Less
Developed
1950
32.9
67.1

1980
4.43 Billion
More
Developed

0.5%
8.2%
8.5%
5.6%
10.6%
8.4%
31.7%
26.5%

Less
Developed
1980
25.5
74.5

2000
6.12 Billion
More Developed

0.5%
9.3%
7.1%
4.8%
6.4%
13.9%
24.1%
33.9%

Less
Developed
2000
20.7
79.3

2025
8.19 Billion
More Developed

0.4%
5.9%
10.6%
4.2%
4.8%
18.8%
20.9%
34.4%

Less Developed
20.25
16.8 More Developed
83.2 Less Developed
as defined in 1980 as a percentage of world total

East Europe & USSR
North America
N W & S Europe
East Asia
South Asia
Africa
Latin America
Oceania

Source: *Fundamentals of Population Geography* by B N Ghosh Sterling Publishers

Exercise B

Find out whether the information conveyed by the diagram totally corresponds to the information given in the text below.

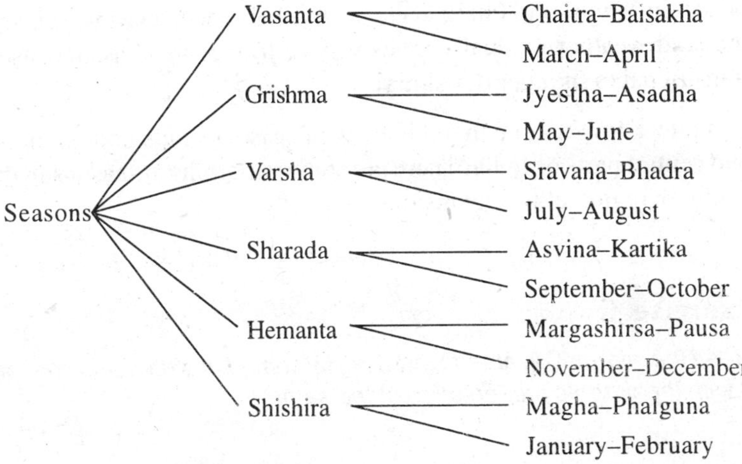

Indian seasons with months according to i. Indian calendar and ii. English Calendar.

Source: General Geography of India – NCERT

According to the Indian convention the year is divided into the following six seasons (ritus):

The Vasanta is the first season of the year and roughly corresponds to spring. The season, however, does not fully coincide with the English months of March and April as it extends over the period mid-February to mid-April. The Vasanta is replaced by Grishma (summer) occurring during the months of April, May and June.

The Sharada Ritu occurs in Asvina–Kartika (mid-September to mid-November). However, there is no clear distinction between the Sharada and the following Hemanta (Margashirsa–Pausa) except that the cold weather is rigorous during the latter. The Sharada is clearly a transition between the Varsha and the Hemanta.

The Hemanta is followed by the Shishira Jyestha and Asadha (mid-April to mid-June). The Varsha Ritu (rainy season) of the Indian tradition extends over Sravana–Bhadrapada (July–August). The rainy season may, however, set in by the middle of June and May and continue upto the middle of September with marginal variations and occurs in Magha and Phalguna (January–February). During Shishira the cold weather gradually gives way to the spring (Vasanta) itself transitional to summer (Grishma).

It is interesting to note that this view of seasons holds good in north and central parts of India. There are some variations in seasons in the southern region of the peninsula.

Source: *General Geography of India* NCERT

Exercise C

Read the information about 'How a digital computer works' and corelate it with the graphic presentation of the same.

How a digital computer works

An input device sends data and instructions to the main memory of a computer. The control unit then directs the data to the arithmetic/logic unit for processing. Finally, the control unit routes the processed data to an output device or an auxiliary storage unit, or back to the main memory

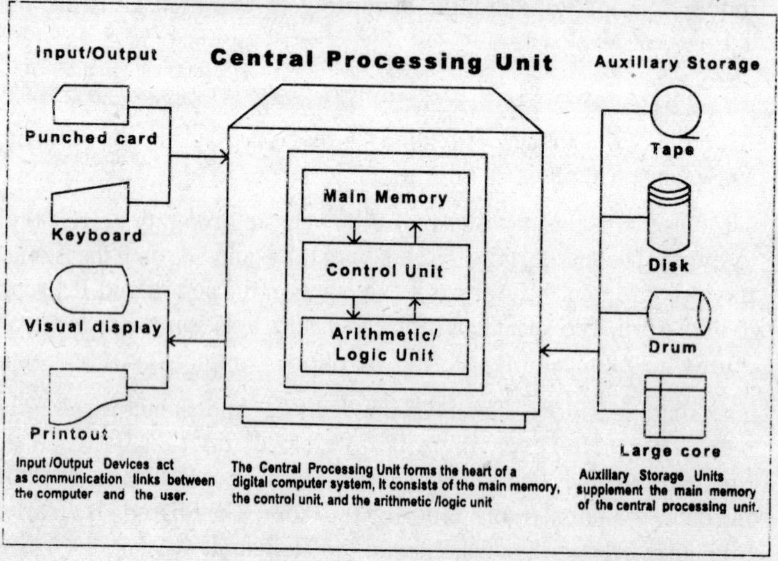

Source: *World Book Encyclopedia*. World Book Inc. Chicago

Although digital computers differ in size, they all have five basic parts: (1) the input equipment, (2) the main memory, (3) the control unit, (4) the arithmetic/logic unit, and (5) the output equipment.

In a mainframe, the main memory, control unit, and arithmetic/logic unit form a single unit called the *central processing unit* (CPU). Some mainframes have more than one CPU, which allows a number of operations to be performed at one time. However, a microcomputer has one CPU made up of one microprocessor.

Input and output equipment function as an *interface* between the CPU and the user–that is, it enables the machine and the human operator to communicate efficiently with each other. Such equipment, known as *peripheral equipment* may be connected with a CPU or work independently of it. If the peripheral equipment is connected with a CPU, it is said to be *on-line*. If the equipment operates independenly, it is *off-line*. Radio signals or telephone lines may link a CPU in one city with peripheral equipment in another city. Such equipment provides *remote terminals* for the CPU.

The Input equipment transforms instructions and data into a code understandable to a computer. This code consists of a pattern of electrical signals that correspond to the 0's and 1's of the binary system.

There are various kinds of input devices. A *card reader* takes input information from punched cards. The pattern of punches represents letters, numbers, and other symbols. A related device is the *paper tape reader*, which senses data from holes in a paper tape.

Most computers have a keyboard that enables the operator to enter alphabetical characters and numerals directly into the computer. Many keyboard units have a visual display, which consists of a *cathode-ray tube* (CRT). A CRT is a vacuum tube with a screen like that of a TV set (see Vacuum tube). The CRT display makes it possible for the keyboard operator to check– and correct if necessary–the data being entered into the computer. Some keyboard terminals of this type have a built-in microcomputer that controls their basic operations independently of the main computer. Input units with CRT displays called *interactive graphic devices* enable the user to communicate with the main computer by drawing a diagram on the screen with a light pen.

Some computers use *optical scanners* to change input data into electrical signals. The scanners optically sense bar codes and marks printed on grocery items, identification cards, and certain documents. Other digital computers are connected to *touch-tone telephones*. By pressing the buttons on the phone, the user can enter data into the computer.

Certain types of equipment handle input information and also function as output devices and *auxiliary storage units*. Auxiliary storage units, or auxiliary memories, can store more information than a computer's main memory but do not operate as fast. The major types of auxiliary memories include (1) magentic tape units, (2) magnetic disk units, (3) magnetic drum units, and (4) large-core storage units.

The information presented in the form of tables, graphs and charts has the following advantages:

1. The data is presented vividly. Tables, graphs and charts highlight the main points and avoid repetition of words and sentences.
2. They require comparatively less space because the information presented is very concise.

3. Precision, clarity and simplicity of the forms make complicated matter easy to understand.
4. They are easy to remember because of their visual effect.
5. Analysis of the information can be done and generalisations can be arrived at without much difficulty.
6. Transparencies of the forms can be used for oral presentations and this saves time and produces a clear picture of the subject matter.

A graph is a drawing which consists of a line or lines, sometimes curved, showing how two or more sets of numbers relate to each other. A graph has a vertical axis and a horizontal axis. Each of them represent an important point of information. A straight or curved line is drawn between these two axes connecting a series of points which represent the varying values of two related items.

Look at the following graph.

PUPIL–TEACHER RATIO IN INDIA: 1950–1995

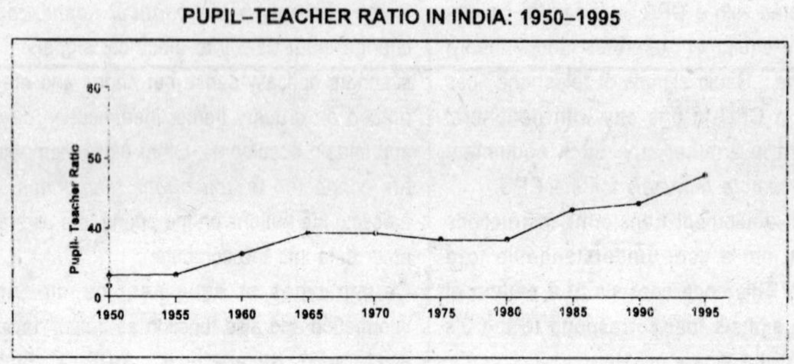

Source: *Public Report on Basic Education in India*, OUP

In this graph the vertical axis shows the number of students while the horizontal axis shows the year. The curved line between the axis connects the number of students and the year. For example, the graph indicates that in the year 1955 the pupil–teacher ratio was 15:1 while in 1995 it was about 45:1

The term chart refers to information presented in the form of a diagram or a picture for the purpose of illustration. There are three types of charts. They are as follows:

1. A Bar Chart

It is a diagram on which narrow strips which are of equal width but of varying height are used to represent quantities.

Look at the following bar chart.

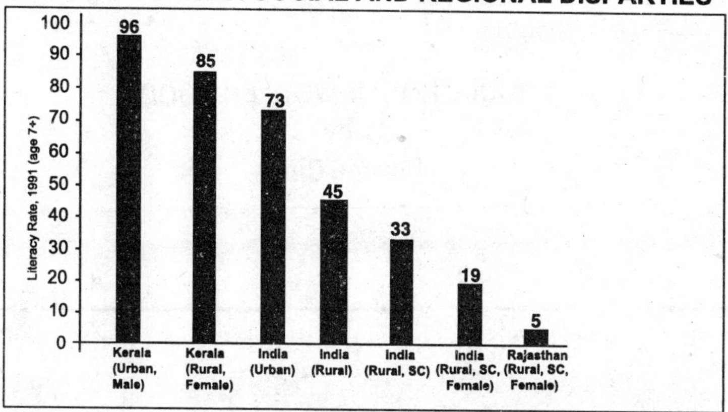

Source: *Public Report on Basic Education in India*, OUP

This bar chart has vertical bars. It can have horizontal bars too.

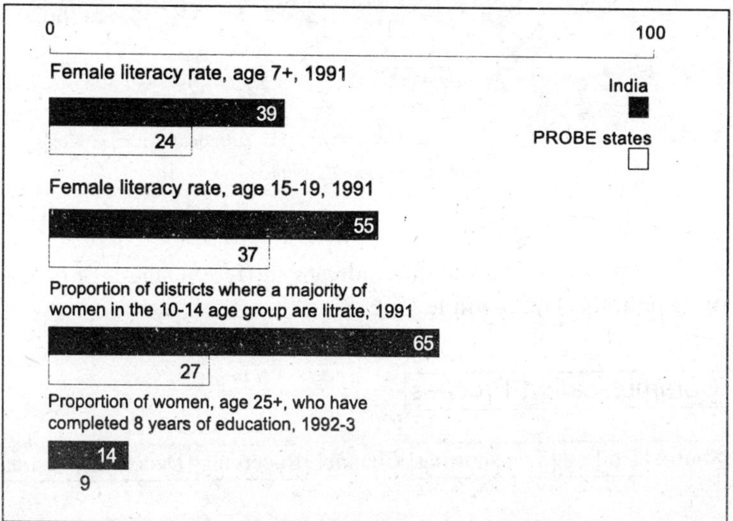

Source: *Public Report on Basic Education in India*, OUP

2. A Pie Chart

A pie chart is a diagram which consists of a circle divided into parts and each part represents a specific proportion of the whole.

Look at the following.

PRODUCTION OF WOOLEN GOODS
by
Divided Circle

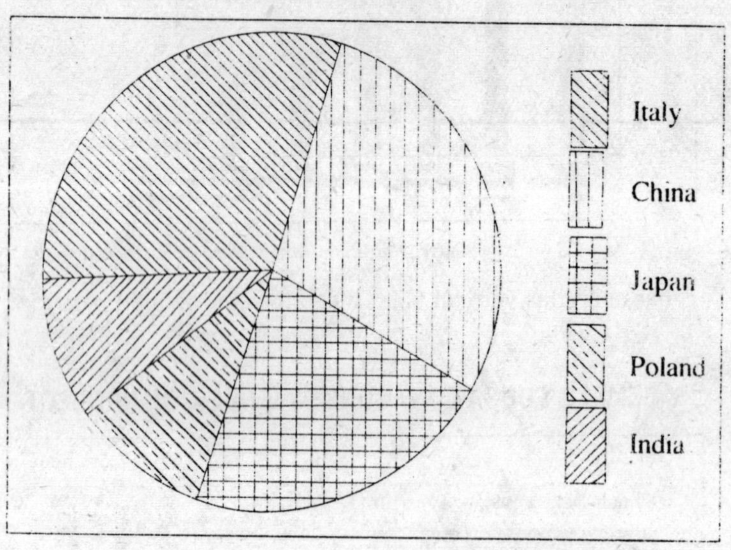

Source *Text Book of Practical Geography* Md. Zulfequar Ahemad Khan Concept Publishing Company, New Delhi, 1998

3. A Flow Chart

A flow chart is a diagram that indicates different stages or processes of something. For example:

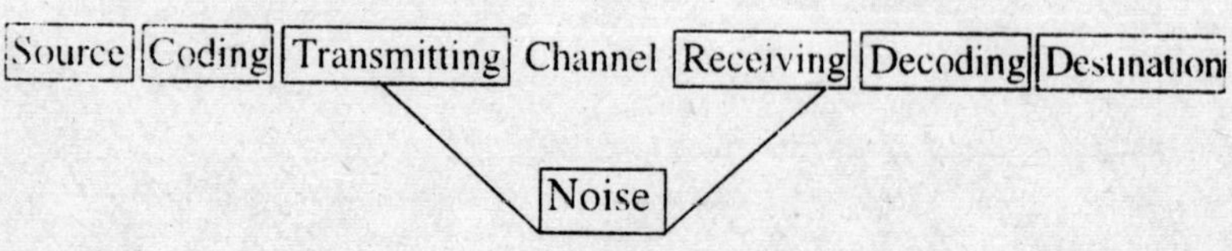

The admission procedure for class XI in a Junior College is as follows:

Admission procedure for class XI

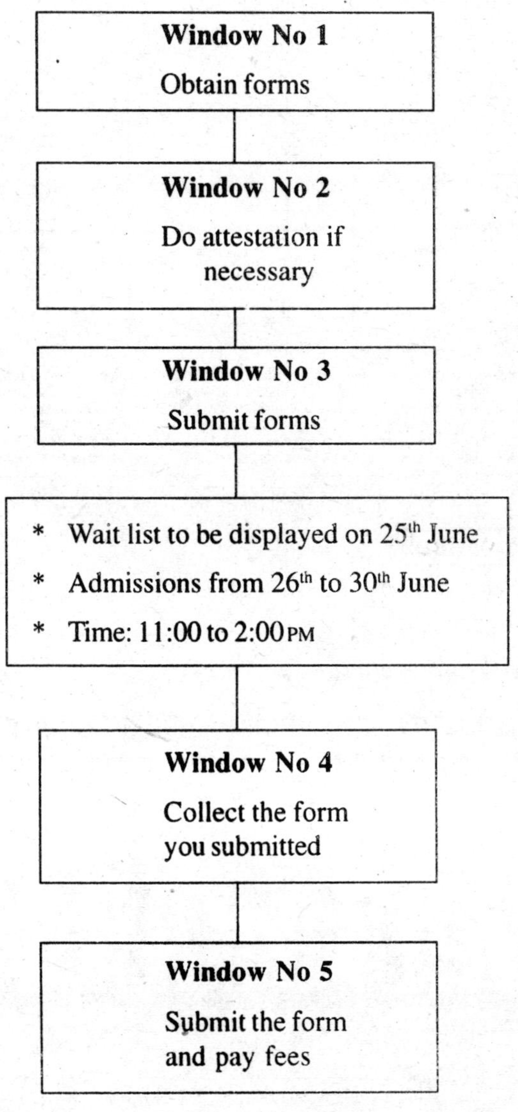

Study the following flow chart.

HOW FLOUR IS MILLED

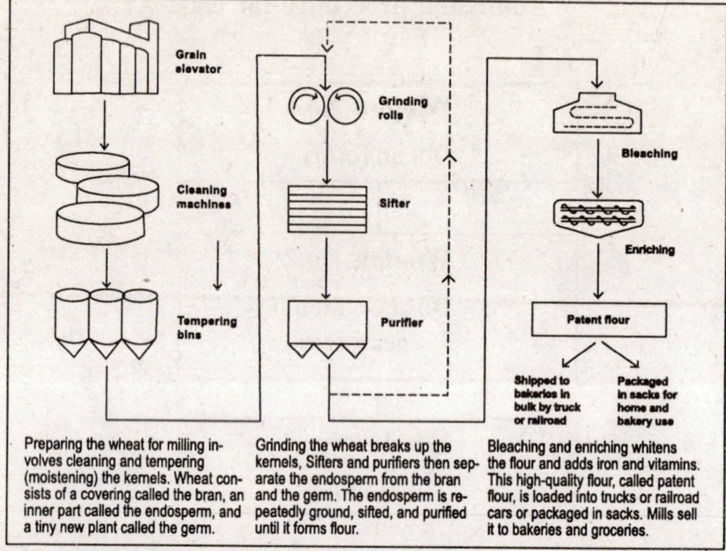

Source: *The World Book Encyclopedia* Vol 7, World Book, Inc. Chicago

Graphic to Verbal

Information presented in the form of graphs and charts can be put in the verbal form.

Look at the following chart.

INDUSTRY–WISE PROFIT MARGIN ON SALES

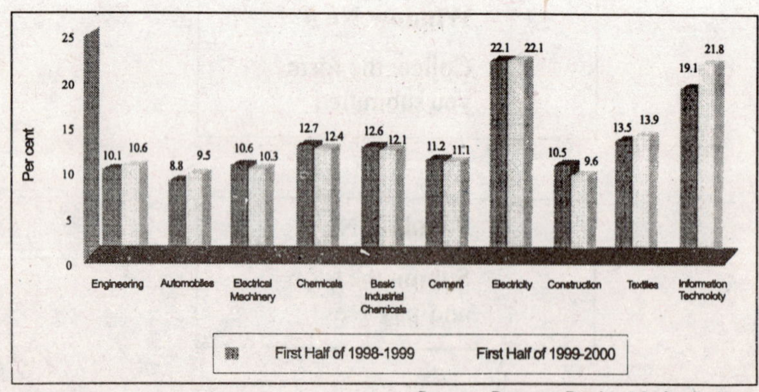

Source: *Reserve Bank of India* Bulletin

The information given in the chart on page 74 can be put in words as follows:

In the first half of 1998–99 engineering industries got 10.1% profit margin while automobiles got 8.8%.....

Thus, you can go on writing down items of information. It could also be just a list of items. For example,

Industry-wise Profit Margin on Sales
First half of 1998-99

1. Engineering: 10.1%
2. Automobiles: 8.8%
3. Electrical Machinery: 10.6% and so on.

You should be able to interpret the graphic information and make generalisations on the basis of your observation and analysis of the given information.

The following questions related to the above chart will help you understand the significant points of information you should take into account.

1. Has the profit margin reduced in the first half of 1999–2000?
2. What is the range of profit margin in the first half of 1998–1999?
3. Which industries get a profit margin above 12%?
4. Which industries get the highest profit margin?
5. What is the minimum profit margin for the given industries?

Study the following chart.

LITERACY RATES IN CHINA AND INDIA, 1990–1

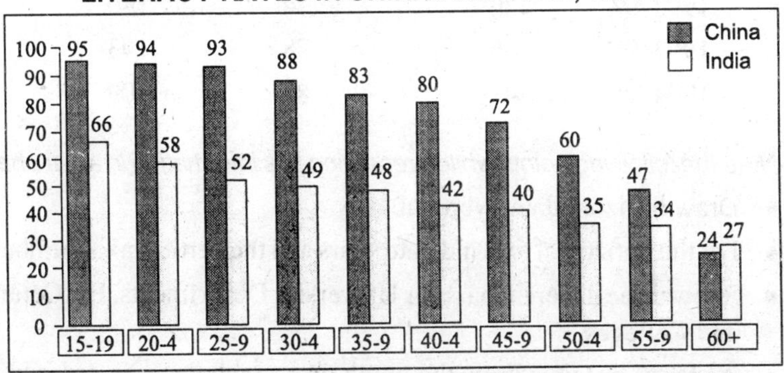

Source: *Public Report on Basic Education in India,* OUP

Note your observations with reference to the following points:

- The literacy rate in China for the age groups between 15 to 29 and 30 to 44.
- The overall average literacy rate of India and China.
- The average literacy rate of India and China for the age groups between 25 and 44.
- The age group in respect of which the literacy rate of India is greater than that of China.

While converting the graphic information into words significant points of information have to be recorded. It is an important skill which demands minute observation of facts and figures given in the graphic form.

Verbal to Graphic

You should learn to present information in the graphic form. Now we will discuss how to draw a bar chart.

The following information shows the number of University Departments, PG Centres and Colleges of the University of Pune during the period 1990–1995.

Year	University Departments	PG Centres	Colleges
1990–91	30	60	161
1991–92	38	72	166
1992–93	36	74	180
1993–94	36	78	193
1994–95	41	85	209

Note the following points while presenting this information in a bar chart.

- Draw horizontal and vertical axes.
- Let the horizontal axis indicate years and the vertical axis numbers.
- Show three different bars for University Departments, PG Centres and Colleges.
- As far as possibie draw the graph on a graph paper in order to be accurate in your presentation.

Your graph will look like the graph shown below.

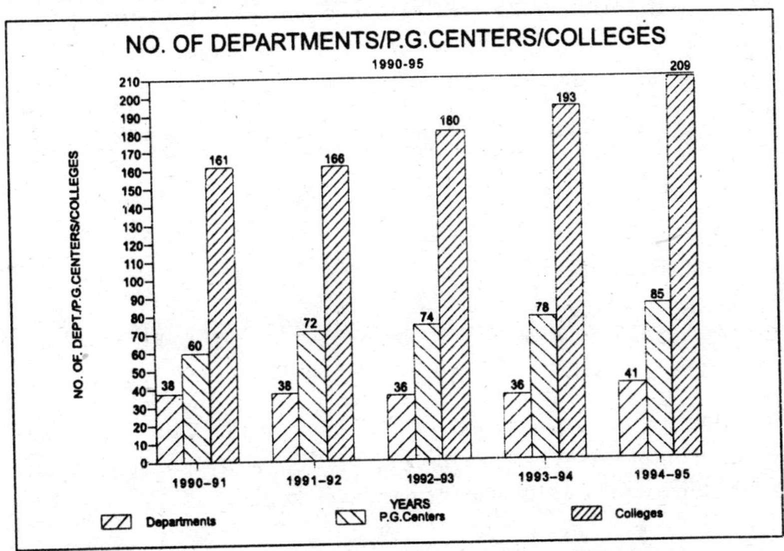

Let us read the following paragraph and try to present the information in the graphic form:

<u>The number of Ph.D's awarded by the University of Pune in Arts, Science and Commerce during the period 1990-1995.</u>

The highest number of Ph.D's awarded in Science (112) were in the year 1991–92 and the lowest number was (64) in 1994–95. While in 1990–91, 1993–94 and 1992–93 the number was 72,75 and 87 respectively.

In Mental and Moral Sciences, 30 Ph.D's were awarded in the year 1991–92 and in the following year. In 1993–94 just 8 Ph.D's were awarded. In 1994–95 the number was 19 and in 1990–91 it was 23.

In Arts, as compared to Science a very small number of persons were awarded Ph.D's. In 1990–91 just 11 Ph.D degrees were awarded while in 1991–92 the number increased three fold, that is 34. But in 1992–93 it was 18 while in 1993–94 and 1994–95 it was 13 and 20 respectively.

As far as Commerce is concerned the Ph.D's awarded in 1994–95 were only 13 which was less by 3 in 1993–94. In 1992–93 the number was 25 while in 1990–91 it was a little less, i.e. 22. In 1991–92 the Ph.D degrees awarded were 15.

Before drawing a chart it is advisable to put the above information in the tabular form which will give a clear picture yearwise and facultywise, and it would be convenient to present it through the chart. So let us sort out the information.

Year	**Arts**	**M & M S**	**Science**	**Commerce**
1990–91	11	23	72	22
1991–92	34	30	112	15
1992–93	18	30	87	25
1993–94	13	8	75	16
1994–95	20	19	64	13

Now let the vertical axis show the number of Ph.D's awarded and the horizontal axis years. Let there be a different bar for each subject. Your graph will be similar to the one given below.

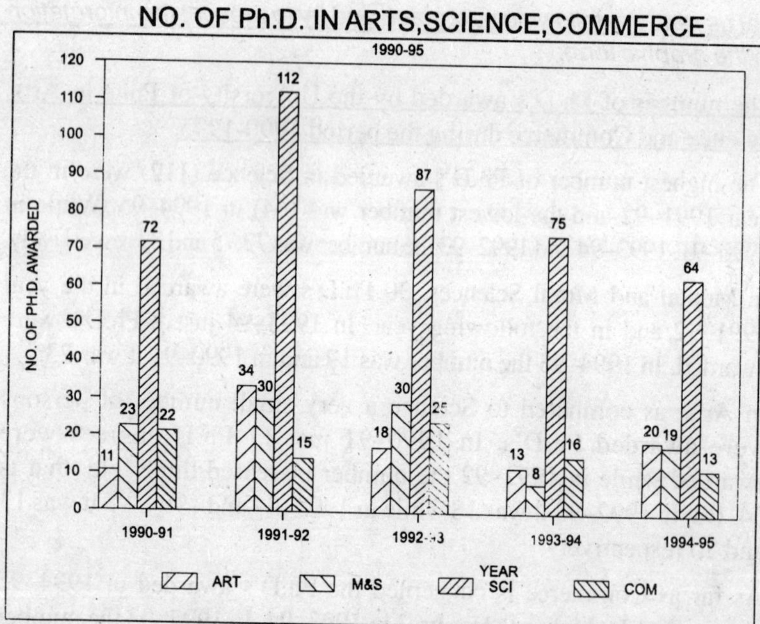

Source: 47th *Annual Repo* University of Pune

Exercise D

Read the following passage and put the information in a graphic form.

The Open University has produced the highest number of audio cassettes for B.A. and B.Com courses. About 120 audio cassettes have been produced. As compared to this, the number of video cassettes produced for BA/B.Com is small, which is 90. More or less the same number of video cassettes, i.e. 82 have been produced for the Diploma Course. In addition, 52 audio cassettes have been produced for the same. The audio cassettes produced for other courses range from 25 to 34—Creative writing 25, Food and Nutrition 30, Advanced Diploma in Management and Distance Education 34 each. The range of the video cassettes for these courses is from 30, to 40—Advanced Diploma in Management 30, Distance Education 25, Food and Nutrition 34. For Rural Development 40 video cassettes have been produced. There is hardly any audio cassette produced for the course Rural Development and the same is true of Creative Writing as far as the video cassettes are concerned. For a Literature course 10 audio cassettes have been produced.

Exercise E

Study the following graph.

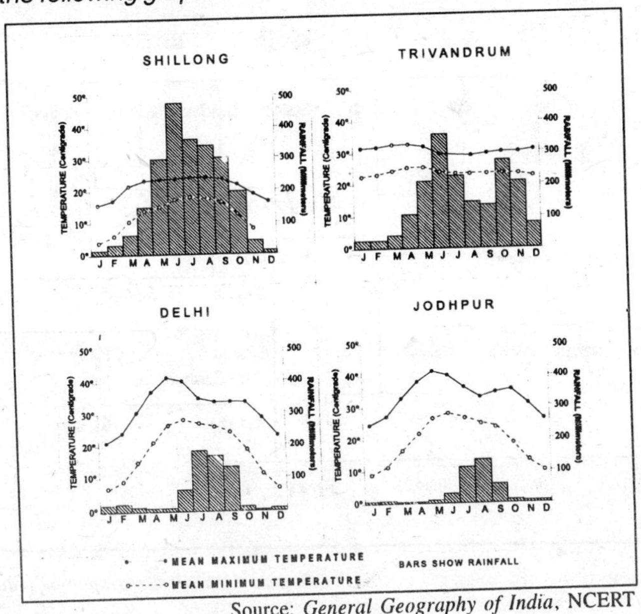

Source: *General Geography of India*, NCERT

Exercise F

Read the following diagram and write a paragraph about it.

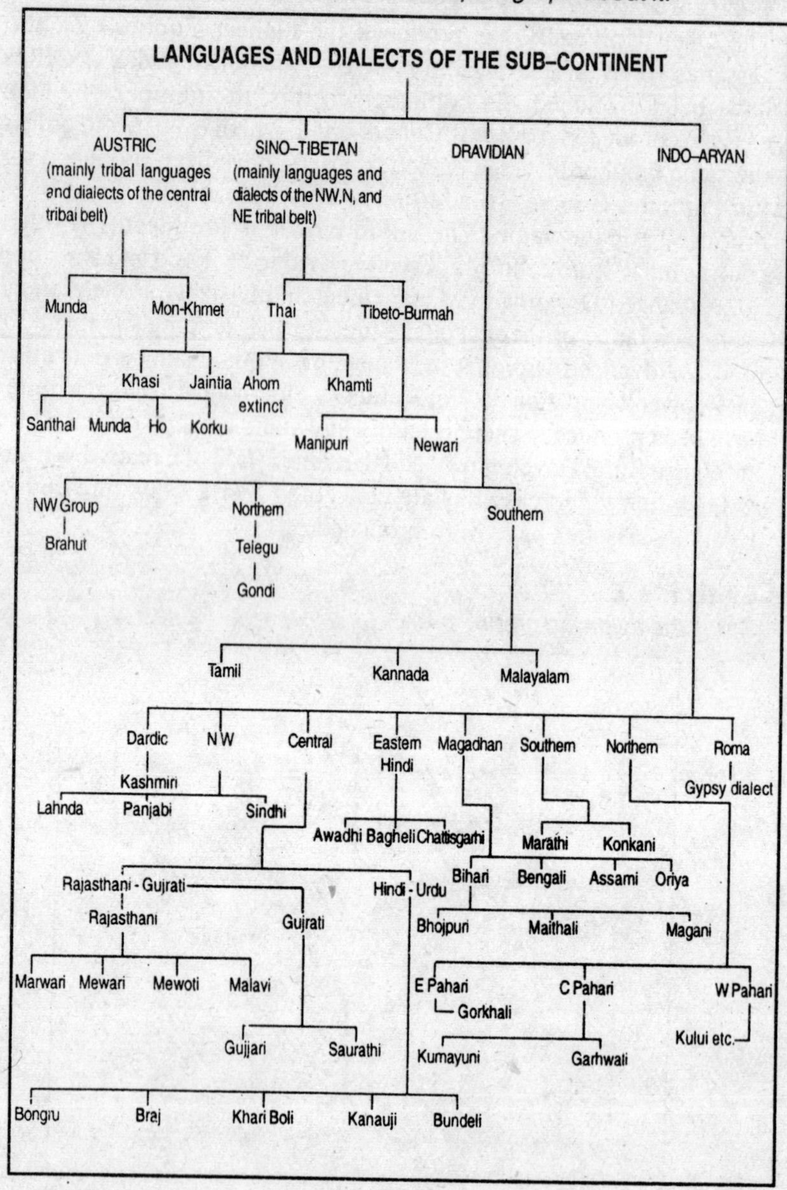

Source: *General Geography of India*, NCERT

Exercise G

1. *Put the following information in a graphic form.*

Tendulkar's 25 centuries

Former Indian skipper Sachin Tendulkar became the first batsman in history to score as many as 25 centuries in the one-day internationals when he made a match-winning 122 runs in the penultimate game against South Africa at Vadodara on Friday. In the process, he also registered his highest score versus South Africa and is now just 50 runs short of completing 9000-run aggregate in instant cricket. Only Mohammad Azharuddin has crossed this run-barrier. May be the last match at Nagpur on Sunday will witness yet another Sachin milestone.

Ten of Tendulkar's 25 hundreds have been recorded against Australia and Sri Lanka (five each), while his highest score was an unbeaten 186 versus New Zealand early this season.

Following are opponent-wise details of Tendulkar's 25 centuries in the one-day internationals.

		Details of the highest score		
Opponent	**100's**	**Runs**	**Venue**	**Date**
Australia	5	143	Sharjah	April 22, 1998
Sri Lanka	5	137	Delhi	March 2, 1996
Zimbabwe	4	127*	Bulawayo	September 26, 1998
New Zealand	3	186*	Hyderabad	November 8, 1999
Kenya	3	140*	Bristol	May 23, 1999
Pakistan	2	118	Sharjah	April 15, 1996
South Africa	2	122	Vadodara	March 17, 2000
West Indies	1	105	Jaipur	November 11, 1994

* denotes unbeaten innings.

Anant Gaundalkar

Source: *The Times of India*

2. *Write a pararaph to convey information contained in the following graph.*

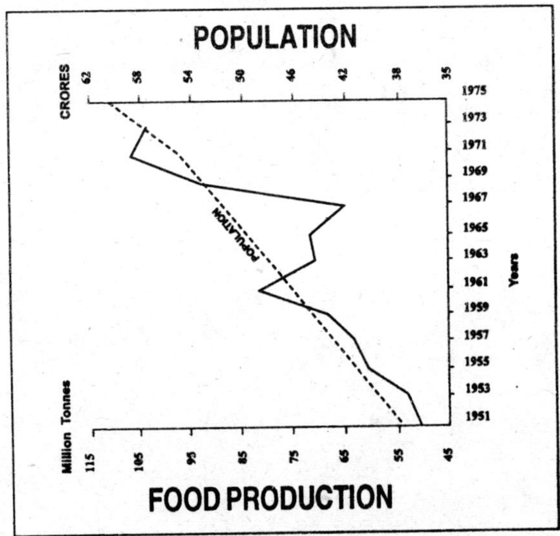

Source: *General Geography of India*, NCERT

3. *Show diagramatically the 'food chain' in the eco-system.*

4. *Show in a flow chart how the items given below are prepared. If necessary get guidance from a person who knows how to prepare them.*

   i. Tea

   ii. Chappatis

   iii. Biryani

5. *Draw a diagram to show how cricket/kho kho/kabbadi is played. Write a brief paragraph of information to explain the diagram.*

6. *Show in a flow chart the farming activities right from ploughing till the grain is packed in sacks and brought to the market for sale.*

7. *Draw a diagram to show your college campus.*

8. *Show diagramatically the structure of the Indian government from the ordinary voter to the President of India.*

SUMMARISING, NOTE-MAKING AND NOTE-TAKING

Introduction

It is always desirable that you speak less but express more and write as briefly as possible but convey everything. In our life, which is ever becoming complex and fast, 'be brief' is a popular slogan.

If you are telling your friend about the book you have read, or a movie you have seen, or something you have experienced, you have to be selective. Omission of irrelevant details and selection of important pieces of information is the principle at work. In all real life situations the only principle that pays dividends is 'speak what is required, write what is necessary.' Whether you are talking over the telephone, or chatting on the internet, or sending a fax message, a telex or a telegram you have to be brief and precise. In any type of commnication 'to be short' is to be sweet, to be long is tiring, boring and time-consuming. In order to be precise, you have to develop the skills of summarising, note-making and note-taking.

Summarising

To give a gist of significant details clearly and accurately is a skill and it can be developed through practice. Summarising is nothing but giving an abstract of carefully selected points of a written or spoken matter. In our daily life we all perform the task of making a summary through speech or writing on a number of occasions. We may not do it in a very formal way, but we do present things briefly in an informal and indirect way. In order to write a summary of a passage:

a. You should do your best to understand the text.

b. After having understood it thoroughly, you should be able to pick out what is essential and reject what is inessential. These are mental activities and they require concentration.

c. The next important requirement is your aoility to use language effectively in order to express the essence of the text. The final out come of these three activities is a satisfactory summary. This shows that the process of summarising consists of comprehension, selection and clear and concise expression.

Read the following extract carefully.

> First, science has obviously multiplied the power of the war-makers. The weapons of the moment can kill more people more secretly and more unpleasantly than those of the past. This progess–as for want of another word. I must call it–this progess has been going on for some time; for some time it has been said, of each new weapon, that it is so destructive or so horrible that it will frighten people into their wits and force the nations to give up war for lack of cannon fodder. This hope has never been fulfilled, and I know no one who takes refuge in it today. (107 words)
>
> Source: *The Commonsense of Science* by J. Brownoski. Heineman Educational Books Ltd. London.

After you have read the passage ask yourself: 'What is the passage about? Well, the answer is 'The passage is about science. The writer is talking about how science has increased manyfold the power of the weapons of mass destruction. Then he tells us about the merciless destruction brought about by modern weapons and says that they may create fear in people so that they would give up war but that has not happened so far.'

This may be the general impression you have gathered about the passage. In order to understand the passage better it would be useful to look for the most important information. Every piece of composition has a subject, a purpose and a tone. The subject emerges from the repertoire of information, experience and imagination of the writer. The purpose determines the treatment given to the topic. For example, if the purpose is to persuade, the writer will use a typical style. Finally a piece of composition is meant for reading and as such the target reader decides the tone of the composition. Thus, it is necessary to identify the topic, purpose and the tone of the text. Particularly in composition like the essay each paragraph has a key idea. The key idea is explicitly stated in a sentence which may be called the topic sentence. The remaining sentences either provide supporting ideas or different aspects of the key idea.

The entire paragraph under consideration deals with the production of destructive weapons and its impact on mankind and therefore this key idea has to be located in the passage. Apart from this, the sentences stating different aspects of the key idea should also be located. For example, in this passage, the very first sentence is the topic sentence 'Science has obviously multiplied the power of the war makers.' Another sentence is '– it will frighten people into their wits and force the nations to give up war –' studies another aspect of the key point . 'This hope has never been fulfilled' is the conclusion of the paragraph which states the real state, that is, the production of destructive weapons has not fostered peace. There are some key phrases, for example: 'can kill more people more secretly and more unpleasantly', 'it is so destructive and so horrible'. You can underline the topic sentence and key phrases.

The next important stage is to express what you have understood in your own words. If you just put together the important sentences or key words in the passage your summary may look like the following:

> Science has multiplied the power of the war-makers. The modern weapons can destroy more people more secretly and more unpleasantly than before. Each new weapon is said to be so destructive and so horrible that it will frighten people and force nations to give up war. This hope, however, has never been fulfilled. (54 words)

Though this is the gist of the passage it is made up of the sentences and phrases lifted from the passage. This does not really indicate whether you have comprehended the passage thoroughly. Moreover, there is still a need to reduce the length and make the summary precise because usually the summary or precis is one third of the original. Let us try to do this in the first draft.

> Science has increased the power of the war-makers by making the modern weapons more destructive than before. This, however, has not frightened people and nations have not given up war. (30 words)

Now, count the number of words in your first draft. If they are more than what is required you will have to think of details which could be omitted from your summary. If your draft is shorter than what is required think of some more details which need to be added.

Let us try the final draft. It could be something like this:

> Science has produced dangerous weapons which can be more destructive than before, yet it has failed to create any sort of fear among people and nations have not become wise enough to do way with war. (37 words)

The final draft thus has to be in your own words but without damaging the spirit of the original. There has to be clarity and directness.

Read the following passage which is a part of the message given by Dr. S. Radhakrishnan to the nation on the eve of Independence Day in 1947.

> Education is the instrument for social, economic and cultural change. If we are to work for social and national integration, if we are to foster moral and spritual values, and increase productivity, agricultural and industrial, we have to use education in a proper way. Science and technology will help us to solve the problems of hunger and poverty, of disease and illiteracy, of superstition and deadening custom, of vast resources running to waste, of a rich country inhabited by poor people. We have to free ourselves from the inertias and inefficiencies which have bogged down our programmes of development. Our administration, at all levels, should become clean and efficient. (111 words)
>
> Source: The Publications Division, Government of India, New Delhi.

Let us first think about the passage in general. It talks about the change education can bring about in our life at all levels. In other words the passage is about the significant role education has in transforming life in our country. The topic sentence obviously is the first sentence. 'Education is the instrument of social, economic and cultural change.' Another important sentence is at the end, 'our administration, at all levels, should become clean and efficient.' Then there are key terms like 'national integration,' 'moral and spritual values' 'we have to use education in a proper way' 'inertias and inefficiences.' Now let us attempt the first draft.

This draft includes all the important points in the extract. However it has to be reduced further. The first draft could be as follows:

> Education is a means for social, economic and cultural change. It has to be used properly for national integration. Science and technology can help to solve other problems like poverty, illiteracy etc. We have to get over our reluctance to work and inefficiencies and make our administration clean and efficient. This is necessary for our progress. (56 words)

The final draft has to be of about 35 to 37 words for which sentence structures will have to be changed. The precis has to be still more compact. Look at the second draft.

> Education is a means of socio-economic, cultural change and national integration. Science and technology can solve our other national problems. We must get over our laziness that hampers our development and make our administration clean and efficient. (37 words)

Practical Life and Summarising: Some Useful Hints

In order to make a summary like this you have to practise step by step. You have to make a rough and then the final draft. You have to struggle with the passage, understand it properly and extract the essence and put it in your own words.

This requires a lot of concentration, thinking, writing and rewriting before arriving at the final gist. It is a time-taking process. But for the sake of practice it is a good exercise.

However, in our daily life we may not have so much time and we may have to do it in a hurry. For example, somebody has written a long letter complaining against your company and your employer asks for a gist of it immediately because he has no time to go through the letter. You have to go through the letter and give the gist of it as early as possible. This is more so with oral matter. You are supposed to attend a function and you are asked to give an account of it briefly. Or you are supposed to discuss some issue related to your business organisation and you are told to talk about the discussion briefly to your higher authority. On such occasions you have to be very attentive while listening to the oral matter, make mental notes (or even written notes where possible), put significant points together, reorganise everything mentally and then produce the summary of it orally (though you could always have written points with you.) Whether you are listening to a lecture or discussion or reading a report or an article, you have to know how to take down notes or how to make notes from what you read. But before we discuss note-making/note-taking let us try to make a summary of whatever we have talked about how to make a summary. In our daily life, there are occasions when we are required to give a gist of what we have read or heard. The skill of summarising is helpful in such situations.

While summarising a written or spoken text you should bear in mind the following:

a. Pay attention to the important points and separate them from the ones that are less important.

b. Organise the ideas or points in a logical sequence.

c. Present the matter precisely and in clear language.

d. Do not explain the significant points or ideas given in the passage. Similarly, do not add your own views or comments on the given matter.

e. Making notes/taking notes and presenting a summary are interrelated since in both the same procedure of selecting important points from the unimportant ones is followed. Thus, a summary can emerge from the notes.

Note-making/Note-taking

Generally, you make notes from what you read and you take down notes from what you listen to. There are some common points between note-making and note-taking. They are as follows:

a. Read or listen to what you have to carefully.

b. Mark the topic sentences, key words and phrases. In case of reading, underline them and if you are listening take them down.

c. Try to establish a logical link between the significant points.

d. The process of note-making starts after you have carefully read or listened to a text. It would be beneficial if you read the written/printed matter twice and then make notes. But for listening, you have to be very alert in writing down significant points since what you listen to cannot be heard again unless it is recorded.

e. Notes can be made pointwise, or in a tabular form, or in the form of a tree diagram. This is important because, whatever the notes, you should be able to reconstruct the main points. For example, you should be able to deliver a lecture on the basis of notes you have made.

f. In S.Y.B.A. you studied how to make use of abbreviations or short forms which you can understand. You should not write notes in full sentences.

g. Making/taking notes is an interactive process. Mentally you interact with the written/spoken matter constantly, try to comprehend the matter as much as possible and write down important points in such a way that you would be able to reconstruct the matter as accurately as possible.

Now read the following passage carefully. We will then try to make notes of it.

> <u>Drug-related health disorders</u> are many and varied. (1) <u>Dirty needles</u> and <u>solutions used for injecting drugs</u> can easily cause <u>abscesses</u> in the <u>arms and veins, liver disease, venereal disease, and infection of the kidneys and brain</u>. (2) <u>Sniffing cocaine and</u>

amphetamines can damage the tissue of the nose and (3) Marijuana and tobacco smoking can cause lung diseases. Heavy users of (4) Alcohol, volatile solvents, amphetamines or marijuana may find that their livers are permanently damaged. Babies of women addicted to (5) Opiates are likely to be born addicted and to suffer from withdrawal symptoms (6) Cocaine and amphetamines can cause hair loss. Recent research has indicated that (7) Marijuana can damage cells. A drug user's way of life makes him more susceptible to pneumonia, tuberculosis, malnutrition and weight loss. Finally, an overdose of any of the sensual drugs can lead to respiratory or cardiac failure and death.'

Source: 'Dangers of Drug Addicts' by Hardin B Jones in *Prose for the Young Reader* edited by D.K. Sebastian 1985 Macmillan.

You can underline important expressions while reading. It has already been done for you in the above passage. the notes could be made as follows:

Drug-related health disorders:

1. Dirty needles, solutions used for injecting drugs:
   - abscesses (arms, veins)
   - liver diseases
   - Venereal diseases
   - infection of the kidneys, brain
2. cocaine & amphetamines:
   - damage of the nose tissues
   - hair loss
3. marijuana & tobacco smoking:
   - lung diseases
4. alcohol, volatile solvents, amphetamines, marijuana (heavy use):
   - permanent liver damage
5. opiates (women):
   - babies born addicted, suffer from withdrawal symptoms
6. marijuana:
   - cell damage

Drug users susceptible to:

– pneumonia
– tuberculosis
– malnutrition
– weight loss
– respiratory/cardiac failure
– death

The same information can be put in the form of a tree diagram:

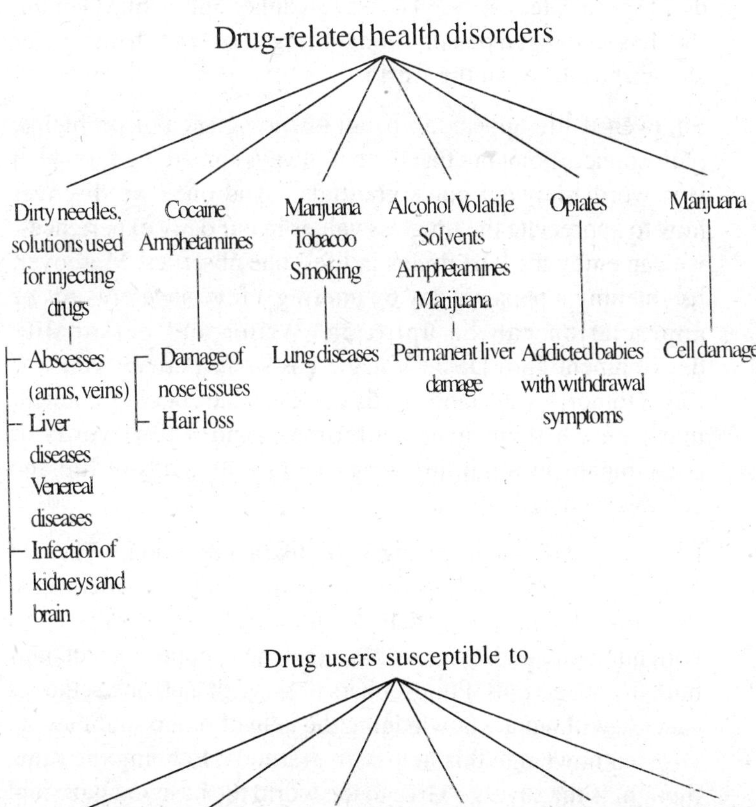

Exercise A

1. *Make a summary of the following:*

   Philosopher and writer of inspirational literature William James once said, 'The deepest principle in human nature is the craving to be appreciated.' To be appreciative of the world has often been described as one way to stay happy in life. While most people feel that their efforts and work are not duly recognised, experts suggest a solution—start complimenting others, or praise that which is good in them. As the saying goes, 'If you don't appreciate, you don't deserve it either.' Mahatma Gandhi, too, has said that a person should bring about the change he or she wishes to see in the world.

   So, even if life appears to be an unending saga of problems, philosophers point out that there is always something for which it is worth showing one's gratitude. 'And once we discover how to appreciate the timeless values in our daily experiences, we can enjoy the best things in life,' one observes. Moreover, brightening a person's day by uttering a few sincere words of appreciation can be uplifting. Writer and personality development guru Dale Carnegie has said, 'Perhaps you will forget tomorrow the kind words you say today, but the recipient may cherish them over a lifetime.' And a few words of encouragement might just help one face the odds of life and achieve a cherished goal.

   It is also observed that nothing works like appreciation, especially when a person is lonely or discouraged. Spiritual teachers have explained that the power to make the world a happier place lies with humanity and it is possible only when people respect their human connections. Philosophers observe that no one achieves success without acknowledging the help of others and that the wise acknowledge this help with gratitude. Echoing the same thought is the saying, 'Give to the world the best you have and the best will come to you.' In his writings, George Bernard Shaw has described the 'essence of inhumanity' as 'not to hate fellow creatures but to be indifferent to them.' (334 words)

   Source: *The Times of India*

2. *Make a summary of the following passage.*

Civilised man is by now well aware of the more obvious symptoms of water pollution: scum-covered rivers, stinking bays, and shorelines littered with bloated fish. The cause of much of it is equally clear: the indiscriminate dumping of raw sewage and industrial sludge into the nearest body of water has exceeded the absorptive capacity of the environment. Because the symptoms of this overflow are so compelling, it seems likely that we shall finally attempt to do something about it. But continued population growth makes it improbable that we shall find the funds to do more than skim off the chunks.

Unfortunately, the most serious water-pollution threats are those which cannot be seen, smelt, or picked up by the handful. The organic content in many domestic water supplies which have been treated to some degree is apparently still high enough to protect viruses from the effects of chlorine. Hence tap water is a suspected transmission route for the alarming rise of infectious hepatitis in the United States today. Moreover, the vast array of chemicals which industry spews into the environment in many cases defies filtration. These chemicals now pervade not only rivers, lakes and even oceans, but also vast reservoirs of ground water. As with air pollutants, their possible toxic effects have in most cases not even been adequately catalogued. Many, of course, are known to be fatal to fish, the mainstay of high quality protein supplies in much of the world.

Source: *Ecocide and Thoughts Toward Survival* by Clinton Fadiman and Jean White

3. *Let your classmate read out the following passage. While he reads it out you make notes from it. (In a regular class, a teacher / student can read out the passage to the whole class and the class can make notes.)*

The functions of universities have steadily increased over the centuries and today they have to enact a variety of roles. These are:

First, to foster the spirit of free enquiry, and promote independent and critical thinking;

Second, to be a repository of knowledge, responsible for its transmission through teaching and extra-mural programmes;

Third, to be the place for the pursuit, generation and application of new knowledge;

Fourth, to be the training ground for competent professionals, including doctors, engineers, business managers and administrators;

Fifth, to render service to society, anticipating its needs and assisting in the fulfilment of social and economic objectives;

Sixth, to promote values and assist in the preservation of culture and traditions.

Source: *University News;* K B Powar

4. *The following is an exclusive interview by literateur V.S. Naipaul to 'The Times of India.' Listen to the interview and make notes. (The interview can be presented in a simulated situation. One student could be V.S. Naipaul reading out answers to the questions asked by the students playing the role of reporters.)*

(Literateur V.S. Naipaul, in an exclusive interview to *The Times of India*, talks about cricket in the grand old days when it was 'a social and racial equaliser' and decries the hard times on which it has fallen. Denouncing one-dayers in particular, he says, 'It's like trying to eat strawberries all year round. You end up by eating rubbish.')

You come from a great cricket playing country, Trinidad, a part of the West Indies. How have you reacted to the match-fixing scandal?

There has been far too much cricket. Cricket used to be such a grand occasion. There were four or five tests a year in each country. It wasn't this constant stuff. Every week there is a triangular tournament. So, the sense of occasion is destroyed, the result is unimportant.

Has this happened only in the West Indies ?

No, it has been a creation of the Indian sub-continent, this overdoing of cricket, this killing of the goose that lays the golden egg, destroying fine cricketers by making them play too much. But it is good this has occurred. It has put an end to the importance of these one-day matches. It will be hard for them to recover.

Was it inevitable that something like this would happen?

Yes, it's like trying to eat strawberries all year round. You end up by eating rubbish.

What are your memories of cricket in the grand old days?

The 'greater cricket' in the West Indies, England and Australia stirred one to the very depths of one's being. I remember those emotions so well as a child. That kind of cricket came from an earlier colonial period. In a place like Trinidad, cricket was a social and racial equaliser. People from very simple backgrounds could play on the same team as the great merchants. And the crowd would applaud them impartially.

Cricket had this extra dimension of social ennoblement and racial redemption. In England, it had the same quality of social equalising. Larwood (the bodyline bowler) came from the coal mines and Jardine (his captain) was something else. Now, in Trinidad since independence, you have racial politics and there is no need for this racial equalising. And people there have gone to games that pay more, like soccer and basket-ball. Cricket is on its way out. To some extent the Black people have done it to themselves. When the West Indies team was riding high, they overdid their racial success.

In what way ?

There should have been some gesture to the White people and the Indians. I'm sure there were some Whites and Indians who were good enough but whose careers were cut short.

But what about Brian Lara ?

Yes, he has been crowned king of a country that's being washed by the sea (laughs). He is sitting on his throne and the waves are lapping at his feet.

What about English cricket ?

There's been a socialist revolution there in the last 50 years. It's a plebeian culture now, which is officially promoted by the 'pop' stars, the football stars, in the newspapers every day. The plebeian sport is football. Cricket is absurd, dead, a game of the twentieth century, not the twenty-first.

What about India and Pakistan, where it is a national passion?

They will probably have to play it among themselves (laughs).

5. *Read the interview given on pages 60–62 and make a summary of it.*

Unit 6

Expansion of Ideas

Introduction

Compression and expansion are two important techniques of developing writing skills. In writing a telegram or in making a summary or precis and in making/taking notes the technique followed is compression, that is, to put ideas and thoughts into fewer words from a spoken or written text. In compression the matter is put precisely and arranged systematically which helps one understand the text clearly and retain it in memory. While summarising or note-making/note-taking the original information, ideas and thoughts expressed in topic sentences, key words and phrases are written down so that they can be remembered or referred to in future. The technique of expansion of a given matter is used in writing a composition, that is, essay writing, story writing, dialogue writing, letter writing and paragraph writing where you are expected to understand and expand certain points logically and convincingly. As compared with compression, expansion is more creative since you can draw on your imaginative power and you are free to express ideas in your own way. The content and the way it is presented are important in writing a composition.

Earlier you have studied paragraph writing. Paragraph writing and expansion of ideas appear to be similar because in both, a paragraph, long or short, has to be developed. However, there is a difference between the two. In paragraph writing, usually, items of information are given in terms of definitions, generalisations and facts and figures. You can also describe something or narrate a happening, show comparison and contrast between something, argue for or against something, and express your own point of view or an opposite opinion about something. In expansion of ideas one is likely to write about the thought content of the given matter. Writing a paragraph on 'pollution' is different from expanding the idea 'cleanliness is next to godliness.' Though the topics are interrelated, in writing a paragraph on pollution you are likely to define pollution, give types of pollution, discuss causes for it and suggest remedial measures to stop it as early as possible. Statistical data related to pollution would support your point of view about it. In expanding the idea 'cleanliness is next to godliness', you are likely to emphasise the importance of cleanliness in our life and how it is as heavenly as beauty and purity. In both paragraph writing and expansion of idea, the difference of content will bring about the change in presentation also. In a paragraph on 'pollution', most probably you would be objective and impersonal while in expansion of idea you could adopt a personal approach. The style, too, may be comparatively informal and at times literary and figurative.

The following specimens will bring out the difference.

Pollution

To pollute means to make something dirty or impure by adding harmful or unpleasant substances to it. Environmental pollution has posed a serious problem to human, animal and plant life all over the world. There are different types of pollution—water pollution, air pollution, noise pollution. In addition to this, there is a lot of visual pollution and also mental pollution. Rivers and seas are polluted by chemical waste from factories and sewage disposal from towns and cities; poisonous smoke emitted by vehicles pollutes the air, blowing horns and unnecessarily blaring loudspeakers deafen human ears; flashes of powerful lights, fluorescent advertisements and gaudy posters strain human eyes. All these types of pollution result from the mental pollution, that is, the negative attitude, recklessness and irresponsible behaviour and antipathy towards public life. The polluted mind that breeds pollution has to be purified first. Right from the formative stage children should be taught that dirtying anything is sinful. If this is not done this planet will be absolutely unlivable.

Cleanliness is next to godliness

Nobody has seen god but most of us accept His presence. God is purity incarnate. Anything pure is close to god — a beautiful flower or the innocent face of a child. For example what is pure, is beautiful. 'Beauty is truth, truth beauty', says Keats.

So godliness consists of purity, beauty and truth. When we visit a temple, the clean and holy atmosphere has a purifying effect on our mind. We get the satisfaction of praying to god with a clean mind. A clean mind is god's abode. 'There is god in us', they say. Dirt creates hell, cleanliness, heaven. Cleanliness makes us fresh. Freshness is a sign of happiness. So cleaning is creating happiness but dirtying spreads diseases. Spitting anywhere, throwing garbage on streets and littering places with plastic throwaways is criminal. All our public places are centres of dirt and diseases— bus stands, crossroads, footpaths, offices, public toilets, gardens and railway stations. Water, a clean breeze of air and a clean plate of food can offer one heavenly joy. Clean roads with clean people appear to be heaven-like. If we do not keep clean, this heaven-like planet will soon turn into hell. Our beautiful earth-mother expects us not to do injustice to her through pollution. If we stop polluting and spread the message of cleanliness and purity the lost paradise can be regained.

While expanding ideas you have to bear in mind the following:

a. Understand the idea under consideration. For example, 'A bird in hand is worth two in the bush', means it is better to be satisfied with what one has than to risk losing everything by trying to get much more. 'Birds of a feather flock together', means people of the same sort are found together. Or, 'A stitch in time saves nine', suggests if one takes action or does a piece of work in time immediately, it may save a lot of extra work later.

   Understanding the central thought or key ideas is significant because you have to expand and illustrate it keeping to the point and avoiding irrelevant details.

b. Think of other related ideas. For example, 'A bird in hand is worth two in the bush' implies, 'We look before and after and pine for what is not'. We are never happy with what we have and crave for what we do not have. To stitch in time (in 'A stitch in time saves nine') one needs to be alert. If one is lethargic and waits till the cloth gets bigger holes in it, maybe even stitching will be of no use.

c. Give examples, quotations, illustrations from history, culture, sociology and mythology to make your expansion clear and interesting.

d. As far as possible try to adhere to the point of view expressed in the given idea. There is no need to highlight various aspects of it. For example, if someone has said 'Good fences make good neighbours', do not contradict it and say, 'It is not true', or 'Fences are unnecessary'.

e. Organise ideas and decide upon the sequence of presentation. Sort out details you would like to make use of, for supporting the idea that is to be expanded.

f. Edit the draft carefully. Check the punctuation and grammatical mistakes, if any. Avoid anything that is vague. Ensure that the expansion adds to the reader's understanding of the idea.

g. Redraft the matter you have written. See that everything is relevant, coherent and to the point. Since the expansion of ideas has constraints of space, one has to be careful in selecting language forms.

How to go about it?

Let us attempt an expansion of the idea, 'Experience is a great teacher.'

Pre-writing Activities

Step one: Understand the basic idea properly. For example: 'A teacher plays a significant role in our overall development. Our development consists of knowing new things and enriching our life. We also learn a lot from our experience. So experience is like a teacher.'

Step Two: Think of the related ideas. For example, 'We study various subjects in schools and colleges in a formal way. We also learn from our parents and elderly persons. Having experiences and learning from them is a continuous process.'

Step three: Think of illustrations. For example, 'How does a child learn to do things ? How do we understand people through experience?'

Step four: Organise ideas and decide upon their sequence. For example, 'The main idea, its implications, relevant examples and conclusion'.

Writing Activity

Step five: Start writing and prepare the first draft.

Post-writing Activity

Step six: Edit the first draft. The following is the first draft. The editing of the draft has also been shown.

Experience is a great teacher

Learning is a never-ending process. Right from our birth we begin to (try to) understand life and it continues through out (till the end of) our life. Schools and colleges offer us education in a formal way (formally). We learn from our teachers, we learn from our (and the) books we are supposed to study, Teachers and books (which) are the sources of our experience for us. We also learn from our mother and father (parents) and relatives (elderly persons). In our daily life we keep on learning every moment (constantly). In course of time, we grow up intellectually and emotionally. We learn how to face new, strange and unpleasant experiences. For a child, fire is fascinating. When the child tries to touch the fire, it realises that it is dangerous (harmful) to do so. In future, the child is careful about anything that is hot and bright. It is only through experience that we come to know the kind of person one is. The more experience we have, the wiser we become That is one of the reasons why we respect elderly and experienced persons (in understanding people). It is the experience that makes us understand life and teaches us how to live life better. From this point of view (In this sense) experience is a great teacher.

Step seven: Make the final draft taking into account the corrections, modifications, additions and deletions made.

Experience is a great teacher

Learning is a never-ending process. Right from our birth we try to understand life and it continues till the end of our life. Schools and colleges offer us education in a formal way. We learn from our teachers and the books we are supposed to study, which are the sources of experience for us. We also learn from our parents and elderly persons. In our daily life we keep on learning constantly. In course of time, we grow up intellectually and emotionally. We learn how to face new, strange and unpleasant experiences. For a child, fire is fascinating. When the child tries to touch the fire, it realises that it is harmful to do so. In future, the child is careful about anything that is hot and bright. It is only through experience that we come to know the kind of person one is. The more experience we have, the wiser we become in understanding people. It is experience that makes us understand life and teaches us how to live life better. In this sense, experience is a great teacher. (183 words)

Let us look at some more examples of expansion of ideas:

Health is Wealth

A person with a bungalow, a car and a big bank balance cannot be happy if he is unhealthy. In order to enjoy life one has to be physically and mentally fit. Even a headache can keep a person disturbed the whole day. Mental tensions may not allow one to have a sound sleep. 'Healthy mind in a healthy body', goes the saying. A person who rarely suffers from any physical illness and whose mind is in good condition is healthy and fit. On account of malnutrition, pollution, adulteration and the ever increasing complexity of life people are hardly healthy. Very many suffer from diabetes, blood pressure, migraine and so on. Even healthy looking persons are very often found abnormal. Money madness is common. Everybody is after money. The value of a person is decided by how much wealth s/he has amassed. The wealthiest person is poor if he has health problems. To exercise regularly, to do one's work honestly and sincerely, to help others and to adopt simplicity is a key to our health and happiness. A person bursting with health and vitality wins the world.

A friend in need is a friend indeed

The saying means a friend who helps one when one needs help is a true friend. In our day-to-day life we come across quite a few persons and we get to know them in course of time, but most of them are our acquaintances. When one is well off and life is green, one is surrounded by a host of well-wishers and admirers. The friend who stands by you like a rock when all others leave you in adversity is a true friend. Whenever one is disappointed or frustrated, a friend is a solace. He is like a oasis in a desert. He makes the journey of our life enjoyable. A true friend is like an angel. Whenever one needs him, even in the most unfavourable situation, he is there to share one's feelings. Friendship is sharing without any selfish motive. That is why friendship is beyond any labels. The only person who can be relied upon for advice, guidance and help in any odd situation is a friend. Though one can be on friendly terms with many, one can have very few friends in the true sense of the term.

Exercise A

Expand the following ideas:

1. Honesty is the best policy.
2. Pride has a fall.
3. Silence is golden.
4. All that glitters is not gold.

ESSAY WRITING

Introduction

In real life situations we express our feelings, ideas and thoughts largely through the spoken medium whereas in academic situations expressing and thinking is done mainly through writing. The ability to collect, select, arrange and use information is developed through essay writing. While writing an essay students are constantly judging, analysing, self-examining and self-correcting. Thus writing an essay can be looked at as an exercise in thinking and self-understanding.

At the linguistic level essay writing helps develop a variety of skills such as playing with words, spelling accurately, punctuating meaningfully, using a range of sentence structures, linking ideas and information and organising the content convincingly.

How do we Write Essays

Writing an essay is not merely adding one sentence to another. You may write very good sentences, but the problem is how to fit them together. The best solution to this problem is to look at sentences as parts of the overall plan of an essay. In other words, instead of beginning with sentences, we should begin with thinking of the entire essay and then break it down into paragraphs and then into sentences. Thus essay writing is a complex process involving the following steps:

Preparation ————> Planning ————> Drafting

Preparation

Any piece of composition has a topic, a purpose, a point of view, and an intended reader. When we write an essay we have a definite purpose like narrating, persuading, or writing an exposition. Our reading, experiences and imagination help us develop an approach which decides the treatment given to a topic of the essay. By keeping the reader in mind we decide the appropriate organisation and style. The following are the major activities perfomed at this stage of essay writing.

a. **Defining the topic**: Asking different questions about the topic helps define the topic and understand its different aspects. Look at the following questions that we may ask ourselves about the topic 'Empowerment of Women'.

   i. What is meant by 'empowerment'?

   ii. What are the weaknesses and strengths of the female sex?

   iii. Do women need generous help from men?

   Question (i) demands definition, question (ii) expects a list of characteristics and question (iii) introduces an argument.

b. **Generating ideas**: Answers to these questions provide us ideas. The more questions we ask ourselves the more ideas are generated. List all these ideas as they occur to you. For jotting down, you can use tree diagrams, tables or columns. Look at the following example relevant to the topic 'Pollution'.

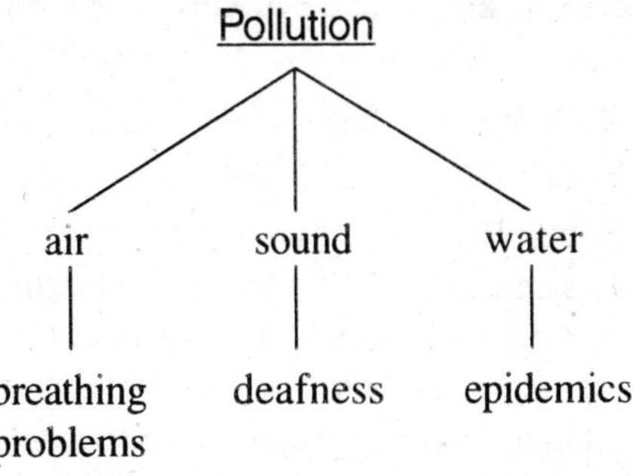

Planning

The ideas thus generated need to be logically arranged. Main ideas and supporting (subordinate) ideas need to be properly grouped together. Identify main ideas and group the relevant ideas around each of them. Develop each main idea into an independent paragraph. This exercise will help you decide on how many paragraphs your essay will have. While planning you can use tree diagrams, a table/column or note-form as follows.

- **Topic**: English in the 21st Century
- **Introduction**:
  - * English as the world language
  - * Spread of English – an overview
- **Facts about English**:
  - * Users of English
  - * English as a window to the world
    - – Literature
    - – Culture
    - – Ideas
  - * Use in business, trade and industry
- **Information Technology**:
  - * Dominance of Information Technology
  - * Role of English in IT
- **Conclusion**

Drafting

Having outlined your ideas as above, you are now well equipped for writing the essay. You have to execute your plan through paragraphs. Each paragraph normally deals with one key point and the supporting information or ideas as pointed out earlier. As long as you observe this principle, your sentences will be automatically linked to each other. A few paragraphs and an appropriate introduction and conclusion make a good essay.

a. **Paragraph writing**: Each paragraph will have a beginning, a middle and an end. Generally you should begin a paragraph with a topic sentence. Supporting information or ideas can be given in the succeeding sentences either in a parallal manner or linked to each other in a chained manner. Read the following paragraphs.

i. 'Road accidents are common in India. → Topic sentence

Recently, 50 people were killed in an accident on Poona–Bangalore Highway. Last year a bus collided in- to a truck taking the life of 30 passangers. In 1996 a bus carrying 60 passengers plunged into a riverleaving nobody alive. Thus, road accidents are fatal' → supporting examples/ information

Look at the arrangement of sentences. The main idea or key point is stated in the first sentence. The remaining sentences give an example each illustrating the topic. Though the examples are not related to each other, they are linked in a parallel manner to the topic sentence.

Now read the following paragraph:

ii. Road accidents are common in India. → Topic sentence

Indian roads are mostly responsible for accidents. Accidents take place due to bad roads and reckless driving. Drivers are normally less paid and some have bad habits. Drinking is one of the major causes of accidents. Whatever the reasons, road accidents are fatal. → supporting examples/ information

Look at the last and the first words of each sentence in this paragraph. The repetition of words helps establish a link between the sentences. It also indicates that the same idea is continued or extended in the succeeding sentence. This kind of linkage is called chaining.

b. **Introduction** and **Conclusion**: Introduction is one of the most challenging sections to write. It has to catch the attention of the reader, establish a relationship with him/her, introduce the topic, set the tone and, by doing that, control the reader's expectations. Let us consider a few examples:

i. The essay entitled 'An Ascendancy of Man' written by Paul R. Ehrlich begins with the following sentence:

'The most startling terrestrial event in the two-billion year history of life on the Earth has been the rise of the species 'Homo Sapiens' to its present position of global pre-eminence...'

Source: 'An Inventory of Disaster' by Paul R. Ehrlich and John P. Holdren in *Ecoside And Thoughts Toward Survival* ed by Clinton Fadiman and Jean White. 1971 Published by Centre for the Study of Deomocratic Institutions Interbook, Incorported. New York.

ii. Jane Austen, begins her book *Pride and Prejudice* with the following sentence:

> 'It is a truth universally acknowledged, that a single man in possession of a good fortune, must be in want of a wife.'

> Source: Austen, Jane *Pride And Prejudice*, ed by. James Kingsley. 1970 OUP, Oxford, New York

Both these introductions not only catch the attention of readers, but also state the topic. Apart from being statements of irrefutable facts, they are put in carefully selected words. Each one of tnese beginnings very effectively indicates what is going to follow.

Concluding an essay is equally challenging. It has to appropriately summarise the essay or highlight the main points. At the same time it is advisable to make the conclusion interesting. An essay can also be concluded with a moral or a striking contrast with something that has gone before in the essay. Look at some examples given below:

a. The essay 'All About a Dog' by A.G. Gardiner portrays the character of an ill-mannered bus conductor. Being a witness to his rude behaviour, the author gives him a piece of advice, and the essay is concluded as follows:

> "He took it very well, and when I got off the bus he said 'Good night' quite amiably."

b. Violet Markham in 'Women In Our Changing Society' writes about the emancipation of women and mentions, in this connection, different milestones/landmarks in history. She sums up this essay as follows:

> 'One after another the barriers about her had fallen. Today she is a free agent as never before.'

Both these conclusions adequately summarise the essays. In almost a scientific manner, a cause and effect relationship is established. We see the conclusion as a natural outcome of whatever happened before.

Reflective and Argumentative Essays

We can classify essays as formal and informal or as long and short depending on the style and length. Essays can also be classified into types as descriptive, narrative, reflective and argumentative, depending on the writer's purpose. In this section we will study only reflective and argumentative types of essays.

The term 'reflect' means 'to think carefully', and 'reflection' means 'a statement which is a result of deep and careful thought'. Thus a reflective essay can be looked at as a piece of composition which is the result of a writer's deep thinking. The main purpose is exposition of an idea or theory developed on the basis of a writer's knowledge, experience and imagination. In this kind of essay, usually, an aspect of a topic is selected and developed or expanded.

The following paragraph can be looked at as an example of reflective writing:

Examinations

> Teaching is intended to bring about a desired change in a learner's behaviour. Examinations determine whether this change has taken place or not and also the amount of learning that has taken place. Thus examinations are an instrument to measure the progress made by students at different stages of education.

Reflective essays generally tend to be philosophical, the writer's perception is reflected throughout the essay.

The chief aim of an argumentative essay is to persuade. It is a kind of a reasoned debate on a subject having opposite sides. The dictionary meaning of the term 'argue' is 'to maintain a case, give reasons in support of, for, against'. In other words, the writer of an argumentative essay intends to persuade by giving reasons. Often a case is logically and forcefully put forward. Debating or arguing for and against is common. The material for an argumentative essay is provided by the writer's knowledge of the facts or reality about the subject and his point of view. Generally, an argument is systematically built and the essay ends with a solution, an observation or a suggestion.

Look at the following paragraph:

Examinations

Examinations are intended to measure the progess made by learners in their studies. But, in reality, they have reduced learners to mere examinees. Instead of determining the amount of learning that has taken place, examinations merely foster rote-learning. The results are mechanical and temporary. Therefore, the present examination system needs to be radically reformed.

This paragraph brings out the contrast between the expectations and the reality of examinations and ends with a valid suggestion.

Specimen Essays

Reflective Essay

ENGLISH IN THE 21ST CENTURY

One of the characteristic features of this age is the dominance and the spread of English in almost all parts of the world. It is being used in all walks of life: education, administration, business, industry, and so on. The fact that two thirds of the world's scientific papers published annually are written in English speaks for the pre-eminent role the English language is designed to play in the 21st century.

The seeds for the spread of English were sown between AD 1600 and AD 1700 , when Britain established its colonies in a number of countries. Gradually the language acquired local colours and spread into fields other than administration. After the colonies regained their political independence, the role and function of English in these countries went through further changes. Because of its use in administration and education, English came to be looked upon as a vehicle of upward mobility, an instrument of progress and a window to the world. The advancement of science and technology in the 21st century has further strengthened the language. Consequently, English has spread to countries like China, Japan, France and Spain where it was not used before.

Today there are about two billion users of English. Around forty five countries whose population constitutes one third of the world population have accepted English as their official language. This shows that English is a language with an inherent strength and has adapted itself to different circumstances and needs in different parts of the world.

Such a language has a greater role to play in the 21ST century when globalisation has made the boundries between countries shrink. Multinational companies are the new business leaders. A need for common code for communication is more acutely felt than ever before. English provides an easy solution to this problem. In fact English has been very adequately performing the role of a link language on international platforms.

The Internet has brought about a revolution in the world of information technology. E-mail and e-commerce are set to change the nature of communication. The language of these powerful tools is English. If these tools are going to radically transform the nature of information flow and human communication in all the spheres, English will have a significant role in this transformation.

EMPOWERMENT OF WOMEN

Equality of men and women has been a subject of debate since ancient times. Various aspects and various effects of this debate are seen in different periods in the history of mankind. Recently we have started talking about the empowerment of women. The term 'empower' means 'to make able', or 'to give power to'. It includes intellectual, social, economic and political power. A woman empowered in this sense can effectively participate in decision-making process and exercise the right of self-actualisation alongside men. Here, precisely, are sown the seeds of the conflict. Share in power is the most unacceptable phenomenon, both for men and women. Historically, man has dominated decision-making in all walks of life and naturally he would like to protect his hegemony. Consequently, all the attempts at empowering women are half-heartedly made. The postponement of the Women's Reservation Bill in the Indian Parliament is a case in hand.

But the real question is does a woman need to be empowered by a man? If real and lasting 'empowerment' is to be achieved, the answer to this question has to be 'no'. Man empowering woman is like a generous millionaire condescendingly parting with a certain (upto acceptable extent) portion of his property. In this case woman will have to be contented with whatever is given to her. The more desired process, therefore, is self-empowerment.

Another question is whether empowering women means weakening men? This question is based an the hypothesis that the main result of empowerment is dominance. This very hypothesis needs to be re-examined. Strengthening somebody does not necessarily mean weakening somebody else. Equality, co-existence, understanding and tolerance are the basic tenets of human society. Self-actualisation and empowerment are to be achieved against this background i.e.,within the limits set by social norms.Thus empowerment of women is a solution to human and societal problems. It should not be looked at as a threat to the existence and freedom of the male population. In order to establish equality, both men and women need to whole-heartedly participate in the process of empowerment of women.

Argumentative Essay

CAN COMPUTERS EVER REPLACE PEOPLE?

Computers have brought about a revolution in human life. To begin with, computers performed certain mechanical functions. But gradually computers took over different human activities. Now even thinking and problem-solving are being done by computers. This has culminated into automation of offices and manufacturing processes resulting in drastic reduction of manpower in administration, business and industry. Speed and accuracy are other advantages. So much is the human reliance on computers that they are being used on a large scale even in fields like music, sculpture and architecture. The growing use of computers in teaching might one day render teachers, classrooms and libraries redundant. This situation makes many of us believe that computers are likely to replace human beings in every walk of life.

But every coin has two sides. However useful they may be, computers cannot replace human beings. Human life is not a mechanical affair. They fall in love with each other at first sight. A pearl like tear silently rolls down the cheek at the memory of a loved one. A compliment by an elderly person restores the confidence of a depressed person. A simple touch of the mother silences a crying baby. Can a computer perform these and many such other miracles?

Nowadays, teaching is being done by computers. Computer-lovers claim that they can learn everything with the help of a computer. Computers also administer tests, declare results and award certificates. But imagine the difference between the two situations, i.e. sitting before a computer and sitting in a classroom with dozens of students around and in the presence of a teacher. The pains and pleasures of companionship; the repudiating as well as encouraging expressions on the teacher's face; the direct interaction, eye contact, spontaneous smiles and abundant sharing and understanding set this living situation a world apart from the lonely, computer-controlled suffocating room.

Thus, despite the many advantages of a computer, wisdom lies in judiciously using it as a tool.

SHOULD ENGLISH BE TAUGHT FROM THE FIRST STANDARD?

There is not much disagreement on whether English should be taught in this country or not. English being a world language of the twenty-first century we need it for communication with the outside world. In the context of globalisation we need it still more. However, the basic issue has been whether it should be taught right from the first standard. The arguments that are forwarded by many against the issue are as follows:

> Doesn't it increase the burden of learning of a child that is already overburdened? When our children are supposed to acquire their own mother-tongue why to bring in English? Children do not have a congenial atmosphere around them to learn English. At home, and in all walks of life, Marathi is spoken. So what is the point in teaching English? Moreover, it is all right for children from Pune and Mumbai but what will happen to those who live in remote tribal areas? And where are the teachers to teach English to hundreds and thousands of children? Many D.Ed. teachers are fresh from their twelfth standard and do not have sufficient exposure to English. What will they

teach when they themselves do not know English? On top of it, what will happen to Marathi? English will strangulate and finally kill it. We will only imbibe into children the slavish mentality perpetuated by the British.

Well, people may say anything they like. What the science of learning says matters here more than anything else. Theoretically a child can learn any language and any number of languages easily upto the age of six provided that language is spoken around the child. That is why, children from the bordering areas of different states happily speak three to four languages. In the existing system we begin to teach English at the fifth standard when this innate capacity of the child to learn a new language is considerably reduced and children have to exert more to learn English. If this is so, why not teach English from the first standard? Teachers can be trained, teaching materials can be produced. English is not going to be imposed on children throughout the day in school. It is just one of the subjects. Even if parents speak Marathi, the child can always pick up some English at school. Children can improve further since they have lot of exposure to English in the form of cable TV. If our children learn English, in course of time they will enrich Marathi more. The earlier they learn English the better they will learn it. This will enable them to face the challenges of the fast changing world where English is being used as a link language.

Introducing English right form the beginning of the school days is a revolutionary decision which should be applauded. The process of preparing children even from the remote areas for the new millennium has just begun. Instead of criticising it, let us accelerate it.

Exercise A

1. *Prepare an outline of an essay on each of the following topics:*
   i. Does education prepare students for life?
   ii. Can equality of sexes really be achieved?
   iii. Advancement of Science and Human Life
   iv. Environmental Pollution

2. *Write an argumentative essay on each of the following topics:*

   i. Will English be relevant in the 21ST Century?

   ii. Does empowerment of women mean weakening of men?

3. *Write a reflective essay on each one of the following topics:*

   i. Computers and people

   ii. Teaching of English from the first standard

4. *Discuss the following topics with your friends and prepare outlines for writing either reflective or argumentative essays.*

   i. Menace of Aids

   ii. Drug addiction

   iii. Women's education in India

   iv. Population and unemployment

   v. Punctuality

   vi. Fast food

   vii. Beauty contests

   viii. Information Technology

   ix. Globalisation

DIALOGUE WRITING

Introduction

Every language learner wishes to be a good conversationalist. A good conversationalist is often able to express meanings effectively and convincingly. He can derive pleasure from the act of conversing and his conversation can be a source of pleasure for others as well. A conversation is an informal spoken exchange of information, feelings, thoughts and ideas. It usually takes place among persons who know each other very well, e.g. friends, acquaintances and relatives. Conversations use speech as the medium of language and are, therefore, spontaneous and unplanned.

A dialogue is a written piece of conversation. In other words, it is a written version of something which is essentially spoken. Therefore, it has features of both speech and writing in it. Dialogues are less spontaneous and more planned. But we need to be careful and ensure that dialogues do not turn into artificial speech. They should sound like genuine conversation. Dialogue writing is a skill that helps us in developing both our speech and writing. It may be looked upon as a preparation for a conversation.

Essential Features of Dialogues/Conversations

The essential features of dialogues and conversations are the same. There are two or more participants in a dialogue and each participant reflects his/her own point of view depending on his/her experience in life. In a dialogue, speakers and listeners keep changing their roles, i.e., a speaker becomes a listener and a listener becomes a speaker. Therefore, one person does not continue to speak endlessly in a dialogue. (A dialogue must not be a monologue. Check the meaning of the prefix 'mono' in a dictionary.)

The shortest dialogue consits of two utterances by two different speakers. For example,

A: May I know your name, please?
B: Rajiv Agarwal.

Of course, a dialogue can be very long as well. It may run into pages. But when we practise dialogue writing, we must ensure that each speaker is able to have his/her turn at speaking and that each speaker's contribution to the conversation is interesting and relevant.

Another feature of dialogues is that they do not always contain grammatically complete sentences. Particulary in the informal style, we hardly ever use complete sentences. For example,

A: Posted my letter?
B: Not yet.

It would be rather artificial to have the same dialogue in grammatically complete sentences. Compare the dialogue given above with the one given below.

A: Have you posted my letter?
B: I have not posted it yet.

The point is that we must not always insist on grammatically complete sentences in conversations.

It has been said above that most of the conversations make use of the informal style. However, the formality or informality of a conversation depends on a number of factors and there are also degrees of formality and informality. The following are the main factors that determine the formality or informality of a conversation.

a. **Topic** or **subject matter**: Some topics tend to be associated with a certain kind of style. For example, if the topic of conversation is 'How to make a compter virus-free', it is likely to be a formal conversation, but if the topic is 'Planning for a picnic', it is likely to be an informal conversation.

b. **Purpose of communication**: The formal style is usually associated with public purposes and the informal style with private or personal purposes. For example, the announcement regarding the schedule of elections on the radio or television is always in the formal style, but if you want to give the same information to your close friend, it is likely to be done using the informal style.

c. **Relationship between participants**: The formal style is generally used when we communicate with higher authorities, our superiors or strangers. The informal style is used when we communicate with our friends, relatives or close acquaintances. For example, if we wish to ask a stranger to go upstairs for a certain purpose, we are likely to say something like 'Could you go upstairs?' or 'May I request you to kindly move upstairs?' However, if we wish to communicate the same message to a close friend or acquaintance, we are likely to say something like 'Why don't you go upstairs now?' or 'How about going upstairs now?'

It is necessary to use the most appropriate kind of-style to the occasion, considering the three factors given above. Remember that approriateness is as important as correctness.

In some cases, an utterance is usually followed by a specific kind of utterance. For example, a greeting is followed by a greeting and a question is usually followed by an appropriate and relevant response. If someone thanks you, an appropriate stock response is 'Not at all' or 'You're welcome'. It is very odd in English not to respond at all to 'thanks'.

Contracted forms like 'I'm', 'It's' and 'You're' are generally preferred in informal speech, because accent is placed on words which are more important in communication. Grammatical items are reduced to contracted forms.

Though we must respond appropriately to what the other speaker says, we should also be able to carry the conversation forward by making comments, offering explanations and giving additional relevant information. Consider the difference between the following two dialogues.

1. A: Your shirt is very nice.
   B: Thanks for the compliment.

2. A: Your shirt is very nice.
   B: Oh, I'm happy you like it. I bought it in Ahmedabad and it cost me only Rs 190/-

It is obvious that in the second dialogue, B offers additional relevant information and tries to carry the dialogue forward. It is likely that A will ask or say something more and the dialogue will continue. But in the first dialogue, B almost closes it and there are no indications that the dialogue will continue.

A good dialogue often brings out the individuality of the speakers. Each of us is a unique individual and has a unique way of perceiving and responding to reality. In order to be interesting, a dialogue must have the element of surprise or shock. That is, a dialogue must not be totally predictable.

Let us consider some examples of dialogue writing.

Getting Relevant Information from the Inquiry Clerk

Rajiv: Excuse me, I need some information regarding trains for Hyderabad.

Clerk: Certainly. You see there are two direct trains to Hyderabad every day. The first is Mumbai–Hyderabad Express.

Rajiv: When does it leave Pune?

Clerk: At 5:20 in the evening .

Rajiv: And when does it reach Hyderabad?

Clerk: At 5:30 next morning.

Rajiv: It seems to be a little too slow.

Clerk: Yes, it is slower than Minar Express, which leaves Pune at 2:30 p.m. and reaches Secunderabad at 11:15 the next morning.

Rajiv: But, you see, I want to go to Hyderabad and not to Secunderabad.

Clerk: But you know, practically it's the same. Hyderabad and Secunderabad are just twin cities and you can easily move from one to the other.

Rajiv: Oh, I didn't know this. Thanks a lot for this information. Are there any other trains?

Clerk: These days there's a Holiday Special train to Hyderabad. It leaves Pune at 2:30 p.m. every Thursday.

Rajiv: I think my chances of getting a reservation on this train are brighter. Not many people would know about this train.

Clerk: I believe so.

Rajiv: Thank you once again for very useful information.

Clerk: You're welcome.

Note that a dialogue must sound like a natural conversation and there should be no element of artificiality in it.

Discussing One's Career

Manoj: You know I am fascinated by music. I would certainly like to make a career out of it.

Rajesh: I can appreciate your interest in music, but I doubt whether you should neglect your studies for the sake of music.

Manoj: So you don't believe I can make a career out of it.

Rajesh: No, I only want you to understand how difficult it is. There is tremendous competition and I know many talented musicians who can't earn their living easily.

Manoj: But do you think I will surely get a job if I concentrate on my studies?

Rajesh: No one can guarantee anything.

Manoj: In that case, I feel there are very good opportunities now in the field of music. Do you remember I sent my cassette to the producer of one of the TV programmes? I have just got an invitation from him asking me to participate in their TV programme. I'll really put in my best into the programme. Maybe some music director or producer will watch the programme and give me an opportunity to sing for him.

Rajesh: I think you are just carried away by your dreams!

Manoj: But there's nothing wrong with dreaming. Let me dream and then let me do my best to realise my dreams.

Rajesh: All right. Best of luck to you!

Exercise A

1. *In the following dialogue only some of the utterances are given. Supply the missing utterances.*

Rita: Is today a very special day?

Smita:

Rita: I see that you have put on a fascinating new dress. You look gorgeous in this dress.

Smita:

Rita:

Smita: In fact, I didn't buy it at all! It was a present from my cousin.

Rita: What was the occasion?

Smita:

Rita: I would like to buy a similar dress. Do you think it will be available in the local market here?

Smita:

2. *In the following exercise, only the first few sentences of the dialogue are given. Imagine the necessary details and develop it.*

Manoj: I think I must go out again to buy some more cigarettes.

Abhay: But you have already smoked three cigarettes. Can't you give up smoking altogether?

3. *In the following exercise, only the first few sentences of the dialogue are given. Imagine the necessary details and develop it.*

Rajani: You know, Prabhakar has just got his fifth degree. He is already M.A., M.Com. and L.L.B. He has just been awarded his M.Phil.

Savita: I think some people are just mad after degrees. I don't know what they do with them.

PRESENTATION SKILLS

Introduction

When we talk to a client about a business deal, discuss with social workers how to wipe out corruption, deliver a lecture on ecological balance, express our views in a conference about the present education system, talk to a group of young people on the evils of the dowry system, or argue in a workshop on rising prices, we are making a presentation. The term 'presentation' means 'to perform with a view to achieving something'. Even if what is presented is a play, a dance, a concert, a seminar or a group activity of any sort, its participants have to perform well and create a definite impact on the listeners or viewers. The presentation has to be planned, designed and executed in such a way that the purpose of the presentation is fulfilled.

A presentation can be in a written or spoken form. The application with a curriculum vitae is an example of a written presentation. How you present yourself in the application is bound to influence the employer's decision. Your interaction with the employer by way of an interview is a presentation in an oral form.

Whatever the presentation, it has a purpose. It has to have an impact on readers or listeners. This is more so with formal presentations. A person giving a demonstration on the utility and functioning of a washing machine has a specific purpose, which is to convince the listener of its usefulness and to persuade him or her to buy it. The presenter of a concert has to make the music pleasant to the ears of the music lovers. A political leader making a speech does so because he wants to get votes from the people listening to him. A biology professor who deals with the topic 'the structure of a human cell' wants her students to understand it in a proper perspective. A cricket commentator wants his audience or viewers to get the exact picture of what is happening on the playground.

In order to achieve the goal of presentation, a person making a presentation has got to be aware of what he or she would be presenting, to whom, how long and for what purpose. In other words, he or she has to master the presentation skills. During the presentation everything matters—the way you speak, the way you look at the audience or the person(s) in front of you, the way you organise your thoughts, the way you modulate your voice, your physical gestures, facial expressions and so on.

Oral Presentation

The oral presentation is realised in a variety of forms. They are as follows:

1. Speech
2. Lecture
3. Group discussion
4. Seminar
5. Workshop
6. Symposium
7. Panel discussion
8. Compering
9. Commentary
10. News reading
11. Reporting

A speech is a talk given to an audience. For example,

She gave a speech on 'Illiteracy in India'.

A speech can be spontaneous. A lecture is a term which is usually used in an academic context. A lecture is normally well prepared and is generally given by a person who is well versed in the subject. It is a talk which gives information about the subject concerned. For example,

Prof. Ali delivered a lecture on 'Indian English'.

A discussion refers to talking about something in a systematic way. A topic could be discussed between just two persons, or in a group. There could be agreement and disagreement during the discussion. In a discussion participants are supposed to arrive at some kind of conclusion.

In a seminar a group of participants, students or teachers discuss a topic in a formal way in stipulated time, usually a day or two. In a workshop a group of people share knowledge and experiences related to a particular topic. But unlike the seminar, a workshop deals with practical work. It is jokingly said that in a workshop 'people should talk shop less and work more'.

A symposium is a small conference for discussion of a particular subject. A conference is a meeting for discussion or exchange of views. A consultation is a meeting for discussion. In a panel discussion three or four experts in the field discuss the topic with the audience. A compere is a person who conducts the programme. She introduces the performers, offers brief comments or observations and functions as a link between the items presented, the performers and the audience. Compering can be done on the stage or radio and TV. A compere has to have complete control over the programme and s/ he is also supposed to know everything about it and its participants. Just as a compere is a presenter of a programme, a commentator is a presenter who offers first hand information of what he is talking about. A commentary on an event or a situation is a spoken description of the event as it happens. Apart from the description of what is actually happening, a commentator can also give her opinion or an explanation on it or even criticise it.

News reading or news reporting on the radio or TV is another form of presentation. In fact any programme telecast or broadcast is a kind of presentation. In a number of programmes on the radio and TV the presenter is not seen but s/he can always be heard throughout the programme.

A presentation can be of one to one type, i.e. a person communicating with another, or one to many type, i.e. a person communicating with a group of people. A telephonic interview is an example of the first while a scientist's talk to an audience is an example of the second. Whatever the type, the principles of presentation are more or less the same and they are applicable to all kinds of presentations.

A presentation has three components:

Planning

A presentation is a time bound activity. The matter to be presented has to be arranged accordingly. At the planning stage the strategy of presentation has to be evolved. For example, when to show a transparency and what oral matter would go with it—whether to have notes with you or not.

Preparation

This includes collecting information, looking up reference materials, making transparencies of maps, diagrams, statistical data, important points etc. as and when necessary.

Execution

It is a realisation of the preparation and planning you have made. During the actual presentation there are a number of factors that come into play. They are as follows :

a. **Confidence**: It is 'the firm trust one has in one's ability'. It is seen through the tone of voice, the way of speaking and facial expressions. In order to improve your confidence you should be well prepared and should not have fear about the audience.

b. **Relevance**: While interacting with the listener(s) you have to speak what is relevant. Bear in mind that relevance is the result of your adherence to the planning and preparation for your presentation.

c. **Language competence**: A good presenter is an effective user of language. You must be very careful in the choice of words, grammatical structures and their use. At the same time you must express yourself with ease.

d. **Clarity, audibility** and **speed**: English has to be spoken with proper stress. This gives clarity to your speech. You should not speak very fast. It becomes a hindrance in the way of understanding. You should be sufficiently audible.

e. **Voice modulation**: As a presenter you must have complete control over your voice and modulate it as required. You should not speak in a monotone. Your speech should have ryhthm. Your voice must change according to the intonation.

f. **Body language**: This includes physical gestures, facial expressions and eye contacts. Movements of hands for example, should be appropriate. Excessive gestures work as distractors. The way you look at the listener(s), the way you smile contribute to the effect of your presentation.

g. **Sincerity**: Your presentation should not appear to be farfetched. shallow or artificial. Sincerity is always an advantage.

In oral presentation some people get nervous. The audience and the general atmosphere creates fear in them. Suppose you go to a rostrum and you are not able to speak because something has happened and you are upset. In order to overcome nervousness in a situation like this, stand quiet for a minute, look at the audience, and make some movements of your hands. This will release your energy and you will feel relaxed. Then begin to speak and slowly you will get confidence. If you are a beginner in making presentations, it is always desirable to keep notes in front of you. You can refer to them when you feel the need to do so.

Specimen Presentation

The functional English students of a college organise a get-together. There are about 90 students. The venue is the college auditorium. The get-together includes items like song, dance, mimicry and skit. Miss Seema does the compering for this function. Let us see how she makes the presentation as a compere. (On the next page, on the left hand side you will see language functions and on the right hand side are their realisations.)

The presenter comes to the dais, looks at the audience with a smiling face and then begins:

Greeting:	'Good morning everyone.'
Welcome:	'I welcome you all on behalf of the Department of English on this auspicious day of Akshaya Tritiya.'
Purpose:	'As you all know, we are having a get-together of the students and teachers of functional English. And I'm particularly happy that all the teachers of the Department and most of the students are present.'
Announcement 1:	'A function of this kind must begin by performing Sarswati Poojan. I, therefore, request Dr. Patil, the Principal of our college to light the sacred lamp and inaugurate the function.' (The Principal lights the lamp.)
Announcement 2:	'May I request the honourable Principal to say a few words'. (Dr. Patil gives a speech.)
Announcement 3:	'Thank you very much Dr. Patil for your inspiring and encouraging words. Sir, you have always been a guiding star for all of us. Well, ladies and gentlemen, now you are going to have a series of exciting items. And what do you think should be the first item? Well, it's the item that will set your feet tapping and your hands clapping. Here is a group dance presented by the F.Y.B.A. students.' (The dance is performed.)

Announcement 4: 'Thank you Shivani for a wonderful dance. The participants in the dance were Kamlakar, Kalindi, Nisha, ... Give a big hand to all of them.' (The audience clap. The presenter waits for a while and takes a look at the items listed for presentation.)

Announcement 5: 'Lord Krishna used to lure the whole world with the divine notes of his flute. Now Akash is going to perform a similar miracle for you and the dhun is – "Savanka mahina pavan kare sor". Ramesh will accompany him on the Tabla. Akash, please...' (Items are presented like this.)

Announcement 6: 'Well, you have just seen the fascinating kathak that brings us to the end of the variety entertainment. I'm sure you all are eager to know whose performance is rated the best. I now request the judges to declare the winners. I also request our respected Principal to give away the prizes.'

(The results are announced by the judges and the prizes are given away by the Principal.)

At the end, the presenter says, 'My friend Manu will propose the vote of thanks'. (The vote of thanks is proposed by Manu.)

Conclusion: 'I declare that the function is over. You all are most welcome to relish the lunch being served in the adjoining room. Thank you.'

While compering you have to take care of the following:

1. Maintain appropriate distance between you and the mike.
2. Don't unnecessarily raise or lower your voice.
3. Be brief and relevant.

4. Use expressions, phrases, jokes, short anecdotes, lines from poems to make the presentation interesting.
5. Highlight the best aspects of a performance from the items presented.
6. Pay attention to time and ensure that the programme is conducted as per schedule.

Exercise A

1. Savita is going to present some items of mimicry. Announce this item and prepare the necessary comments. You could talk a little about Savita. Write down the comments and practise saying them aloud.
2. Prepare a news bulletin regarding happenings in your Department or College. Make the news items humorous. For example, 'there is news that Akshay has finally succeeded in attending his first lecture of the year and that happens to be the last lecture for the others.'

   Write down such news items and appropriate comments for each of them.
3. There is an inauguration of the library building of your college. You are the compere. Imagine all the necessary details and prepare your script for compering.
4. Select any topic from your special subject and prepare a short presentation for about five minutes for those who do not know that subject. Prepare material for transparencies or handouts.
5. You have visited a place of historical, cultural or geographical importance during your study tour. You have discussed a few things related to your curriculum. Present a written or oral report on the tour to your teacher.
6. Imagine that there is an interview for a managerial post. At the end of the interview the interviewers tell you to make a presentation to prove that you are the most eligible candidate for the said post. Prepare a presentation.

INTERVIEW

Introduction

An interview is a kind of presentation. There are different kimds of interviews. In a job interview the person who is interviewed, i.e., the interviewee or the candidate is asked questions by person(s) interviewing, i.e., interviewers. There is another kind of interview where a reporter puts questions to the person interviewed in order to get information or the person's views on something. Whatever the type, the interviewee has to perform well in order to create an impression on the interviewers. In this unit will consider job interviews, how to prepare for them, how to face them and what, in general, are the parameters on the basis of which a candidate is selected for a particular position.

Aspects of an Interview

Though the criteria for selection vary from job to job there are some common criteria irrespective of the kind of job for which the interview is held. They are as follows:

1. Physical Appearance

On a personality scale, these days, one's physical appearance is placed almost at the end. 'Handsome is what handsome does' goes the saying, which means that a person can be judged from his performance and behaviour, not from his appearance. One's personality gets expressed in his/her performance. For example, a TV news reader's personality is not how she looks but how she reads out the news.

It does not mean that you should be careless about your appearance. You should be clean and fresh, wear clean, ironed clothes to make a favourable first impression. You should be lively, alert, polite and be able to respond quickly and appropriately. It is the quality of the mind that matters rather than the clothes you wear. As regards clothes the guiding principle here is 'you should wear clothes that suit you'. The dress you wear should make you look normal, natural and pleasant. It should certainly not be gaudy or unusually 'bold'. In short, you should be presentable. If you are a male candidate, your hair style should be moderate and your shoes should be polished. If you are a female candidate you should not overuse cosmetics. An interviewee, in any case, should not look clumsy.

Some positions, like public relations officer, for example, expect the candidate to have an 'impressive personality.' For most of the jobs the person applying is expected to be healthy in body and mind.

2. Positive Attitude to Life

For most of the interviews for responsible posts, usually there is a psychologist sitting among the interviewers who observes the candidate's behaviour and gives an estimate about the candidate's mental make-up to the employer concerned. A candidate who has a positive attitude to life, who is optimistic and encouraging has always got an advantage over other competitors. The person who believes that misfortunes, failures, defeats are not the end of the world has a positive attitude. A person certainly has a positive attitude if s/he believes that there is no problem in the world which does not have at least two solutions. A person with a positive attitude always feels that there is always a room at the top and nothing is late. Positivism is looked upon as a plus point and many people seem to have become aware of it. Imagine during an interview for an a officer's post you are asked a question like, 'what are your strong points?' The answer you give will indicate whether you are positive in your approach or not. One of the likely answers could be:

> 'I'm capable of making use of my power and I can always get the things done whatever the circumstances. I'm not afraid of anyone. I can put a person straight in no time if he is not punctual or is negligent of his responsiblities.'

An answer that will make a far better impact on the interviewers could be something like this:

> 'I can understand people and their problems better. Therefore, I can make people work willingly. I exercise my powers only when I'm required to. I can get along with people and that saves a lot of energy. I believe in conciliation and compromises rather than encounters. I find pleasure in working and I can work for hours. I hate postponing anything that I can do now.'

3. Clarity of Thought and Logic

Confused thinking is a symptom of a chaotic mind. The interviewers would always like to find out whether you can think clearly and logically. Lak of clarity in thought results from a confused mind and is likely to lead to undesirable consequences. A logical mind, that is, a mind with the ability to relate a cause with its effect is the demand if the computer dominated society. Suppose you are selling a mixer-cum-grinder of a particular company and the customer asks you 'What's so special about this mixer?' Your answer cannot be vague or longwinding such as,

> 'You know, it is manufactured by a well-known company. There are many mixers available in the market today but show me one mixer of this kind. This is unique. Look at its colour and shape. If you want to buy a mixer, go for this. I can give you a guarantee. It is not available with any other shopkeeper in the city'.

Of course, only an untrained or inexperienced salesperson can speak like this about the product s/he is selling. A good, professional salesperson will say,

> 'Well, the latest Japanese technology is behind the making of it. Its motor is stronger than that of any other mixer and yet it uses far less electricity than any of them. It is very safe, moderately priced and has more accessories than others of its kind. It's very durable and has rust-proof detachable blades. Aboveall, we have various instalment schemes for your convenience'.

If you are a marketing manager, you should be in a position to observe the market situation, analyse it, assess it and accordingly make suggestions. If your logic is weak, observation poor and analysis unscientific, results would be unfavourable and to your disadvantage.

4. Professional Skill

A skill or expertise required for a particular profession will vary from one profession to another. If you are going to be a computer operator you have to know how to operate a computer. If you are a programmer, then you are supposed to prepare the relevant software. As a manager, you should have the ability to get along with people and get the work done. You also have to take decisions in the interest of the organisation you work in. If you are a salesperson, you have to be very persuasive while as a police officer you have to be comparatively stern. The employer would always look for the necessary professional skills in the interviewee. If you have the required skills let the prospective employer know that you have them.

5. Ability to Communicate:

Some professions like teaching and marketing demand fluency and command over language. As far as English is concerned the interviewee has to pay attention to pronunciation. The English spoken by you should not be coloured by your mother tongue. The expressions you use should be appropriate. A natural way of speaking is preferable to a farfetched imitation of the native speaker. You should also know the strategies of conversation, for example, if you wish to disagree on some point with the interviewer you shoud do so in a polite but firm manner. She may say 'Well, our country is a country of farmers. 80% people live in villages and their main occupation is farming. So I think we really don't need English. Why to impose English on masses? What's your opinion?' If you do not agree with this, while responding to a question like this you could say, 'What you say is right but …../ I agree with you but …../ You have a significant point but …./ True but ……/ That's right but …… We do need English for other reasons.'

Preparing for the Interview

You should prepare for an interview with the following points in mind. How would you go about it?

1. Take a Look at the Advertisement and the Interview Call Letter

Carefully read the advertisement in response to which you have applied. Keep with you the copy of the application you sent. Take a look at the call letter. Note the time and the venue of the interview. You have to know about the place you have to go to. Depending on the distance, you have to decide how you would be reaching the spot and in order to reach in time, when to start and how – by bus, train or car? If it is in a different town or a far off place, then you will have to plan accordingly. It is always better to have the address of the office with the telephone number in your diary.

2. Revise the Subject

Whatever job you have applied for you should be able to anticipate the questions that could be asked during the interview. May be, you will have to consult experts or experienced persons in the field. Probably you will have to consult reference books. But all this will depend on the job for which you have applied.

3. Decide on the Dress to wear

As has already been pointed out, the dress has to be the one you find yourself most comfortable in and which is appropriate for the occasion. You also have to think of the bag you will be carrying with you. If you are a male candidate, you may have to put on a tie if the position requires it.

4. Take Necessary Certificates and Testimonials

You will have to make sure that you have all the certificates, original as well as photocopies, in your file. Sometimes a 'character certificate' or 'experience certificate,' if you have any previous experience, is required. If you have published articles on the subject concerned or have photographs or accounts of what you have done. take it with you.

5. Be Confident

Have confidence in yourself. Say to yourself that you will face the interview successfully. You can imagine yourself facing the actual interview–the way you would be entering the room, the way you would greet the interview panel, the way you would be responding to the interviewers, the kind of language and body language you are likely to use.

At the Time of the Interview

1. Reach the Place of Interview in Time

Start sufficiently early from home. Make sure you have taken with you all the required papers. You also have with you the call letter, the address of the venue and the phone number.

2. After Reaching the Place of Interview

It is always better to be at the place of interview fifteen minutes before the time of the interview. Before actually attending the interview you can make yourself at home with the environment. If necessary, you can find out from someone there where the WC is and have a wash which will make you fresh. Here, make use of the English you have learned. You can make use of various ways of making a request: 'Could you plcase tell me where the WC is?'/ 'Would you mind telling me where the WC is?'/'Excuse me, please tell me where the WC is?'/'Excuse me, but is there a WC around ?' If you are not the first candidate, you can interact with the person who has already done the interview. You could find out, for example, the seating arrangement, the number of interviewers and so on. If you come to know some unexpected things do not get upset.

3. After you Enter the Room

When you are called for the interview don't run or walk fast because your breathing will be fast and speaking could be a problem. You are likely to falter then. May be you will be at a loss for words or you may look clumsy while speaking. So before entering, keep cool, walk in slow but steady. Keep yourself impressive, look confident and tell yourself that you will do your best.

While entering say 'May I come in sir?' After you reach the interviewers do not occupy the chair immediately. Say 'Good morning/

afternoon/evening'. and sit only after you are told to. Sit comfortably and be at ease, keep the file of your papers on the table.

4. While Answering the Questions

The interviewers are likely to ask you for some personal information. For example, they might want to confirm the information you have given in your application. Therefore there should not be any discrepancy between the information you have put in your application and the information you would be supplying now. Have a gentle smile on your face while answering.

One of the questions that is usually asked during any interview is 'Why have you applied for this job?' or 'Why are you interested in this position?' and your answer should be wise. If you just say 'Because I like it', it does not mean much. Avoid vague answers like this. Another usual question is , if it is not mentioned in the ad, 'How much salary do you expect?' If it is a private organisation you could say, for example, 'Well I believe my worth is 25000/- a month but it can always be decided after you see my work.'

Don't forget that every action, response, expression is constantly observed by a psychologist as has already been pointed out. You should not show signs of nervousness or a sense of diffidence or loss of confidence. In answering the question you should be clear and direct. If you cannot answer the question say ' Sir(s), I'm sorry I do not know about it'. Saying this is always preferred to giving a tentative answer. While interacting with the interviewers do not make uncalled for movements of your hands or legs. For example, do not run your fingers through your hair or do not take your hand to your mouth, nose or ears. Sit straight and appear pleasant. At the end, say 'Thank you' and get out gracefully.

5. A Final Piece of Advice

Employers prefer enthusiastic and dynamic persons. Particularly in the corporate sector a result-oriented and hard-working person is preferred. A person with strong determination, discipline and sincerity has a lot of scope. Getting along with people and getting things done is a new value. Any industrial unit, company or business organisation will never hesitate to invest in you if you are worth it.

Specimen Interview

Here is a sample interview held for the post of a lecturer in English at a Junior College. The interviewee has already entered the room and is sitting in a chair. The interviewers begin to interact with her.

On the left side of this page you will find what happens during the interview and on the right side there are observations, comments and useful hints mainly from the language and usage point of view.

Interviewer 1: Interviewee:	May I know your name? I'm Vasanti Patil.	You could also say, 'Vasanti Patil' Do not say 'My name is Vasanti Patil.' It sounds schoolish. Moreover, the interviewer already knows your full name but just wants to confirm it. The interviewers know your marital status from your application. Avoid saying 'I'm Miss Vasanti Patil.'
Interviewer 1: Interviewee:	Tell us about your qualifications. I did B.A. English from KTHM College Nashik in 1996. I stood first in the college with 62% marks. In 'The structure of Modern English' I've got 87%. For my M.A. I was with the University. In M.A. also I've maintained the first class.	The interviewer has all the information about your educational qualifications in your application and would check it with the information you are giving now. Mention the distinctions you have achieved.

Interviewer 1: Interviewee:	Do you have any experience of teaching ? Not really. But I've been giving tuitions to XI and XII class students. So I believe I know what it is to teach.	 You have to be tactful here. You do not have any teaching experience. However, you can always cash in on what you have done which is similar to teaching.
Interviewer 2: Interviewee:	Why do you want to be a teacher ? It is the teacher who comes in contact with the new generation every year. She knows their dreams, desires and problems. A teacher is always in touch with knowledge. As a teacher I would like to be a part of the making of the youth. So I like teaching.	 Here you have to justify why you like the profession. You have to be logical, realistic and convincing. A stock answer like 'I want to be a teacher because teaching is a noble profession', does not make any impression.
Interviewer 3: Interviewee:	Could you tell us about the qualities of a good teacher ? A good teacher is a great lover of knowledge. It is her passion. A teacher has to be a good human being. She has love for her students. A teacher is encouraging and inspiring. She has the ability to give her students something beyond books She is a good communicator.	 Be brief and to the point. Avoid vague answers. It would be safe not to say something like 'A teacher should have an impressive personality and she should speak very fluently'.

Interviewer 4 :	Do you think you have those qualities? Are you fit to be a good teacher?	
Interviewee:	I may not have all the qual'ties a good teacher is expected to have. But to be a good teacher is my dream and I'll always try to bring the dream into practice. I'm aware of my limitations but great teachers like Tilak, Tagore and Radhakrishnan are my ideals.	While responding to a question like this, do not show off. Claiming to have all the qualities of a good teacher shows over-confidence which may sound rude. Be moderate and sincere in your answers.
Interviewer 5:	You said you take tuitions. How much Marathi do you use in teaching English?	
Interviewee:	Very little. Because, I believe, if I use Marathi that will deprive students of their exposure to English. The more the exposure the more the learning is the principle of language learning. But I use Marathi sparingly.	The question is rather tricky. Do not give the usual answer which is 'I use Marathi because otherwise students do not understand English'.
Interviewer 5:	What do you think is the aim of teaching English?	
Interviewee:	To teach students how to make use of English in their day-do-day life in different situations. It should make them good readers, good listeners and effective communicators.	Again, the question is not easy. It is going to test your theoretical knowledge i.e. principles of language teaching and learning.

Interviewer 5: Interviewee:	What is important? What the teacher teaches or what the students learn? I suppose, whatever the teacher does in the classroom is significant as long as it helps students learn English. If students don't learn anything, teaching, however good it may be, is of no use.	 Be polite and tactful. Highlight the process of learning that should be activated by the teacher.
Interviewer 5: Interviewee:	Good. We will communicate our decision shortly. Thank You. Thank you sirs. (Goes out)	Don't make the mistake of asking 'When are you likely to communicate your decision?' This is unwarranted.

Exercise A

1. Imagine that you are facing an interview for a Junior college lecturer in Marathi/Hindi/History/Political Science/Geography/ Economics/Sociology.
   Anticipate about 8 to 10 questions and write down your possible responses.
2. Imagine that you are starting a business and you have applied for a loan from a bank. The bank authorities interview you for the loan to be sanctioned.
   Think of 8 to 10 probable questions and write down your response.
3. You have applied for a scholarship for studying abroad. You have been short-listed and your final selection will depend on your successful performance in the interview by the authorities concerned.
   Imagine about 8 to 10 questions and prepare your response.
4. Imagine that you are facing an interview for the post of Deputy collector/DYSP/Finance Officer/PSI/Taheshildar.
   Write down how you would prepare for the interview.